Premiere

On the Runway

Melody Carlson

BOOK ONE

Ζ ZONDERVAN®

ZONDERVAN.com/
AUTHORTRACKER
follow your favorite authors

ZONDERVAN

Premiere
Copyright © 2010 by Melody Carlson

This title is also available as a Zondervan ebook.
Visit www.zondervan.com/ebooks.

Requests for information should be addressed to:
Zondervan, *Grand Rapids, Michigan* 49530

Library of Congress Cataloging-in-Publication Data

Carlson, Melody.
    Premiere / Melody Carlson.
        p.   cm. — (On the runway ; bk. 1)
        Summary: When two sisters get their own fashion-focused reality
television show, vivacious Paige is excited, but Erin, a Christian who is more
interested in being behind the camera than in front of it, has problems with
some of the things they are asked to do.
        ISBN 978-0-310-71786-7 (softcover)
        [1. Reality television programs — Fiction. 2. Television — Production and
direction — Fiction. 3. Fashion — Fiction. 4. Sisters — Fiction. 5. Interpersonal
relations — Fiction. 6. Christian life — Fiction.] I. Title.
    PZ7.C216637Pn 2010
    [Fic] — dc22
                                                              2009048438

Art direction: Michelle Lenger
Cover design: Connie Gabbert, Faceout Studios
Interior design & composition: Patrice Sheridan, Carlos Eluterio Estrada &
Tina Henderson

Printed in the United States of America

10 11 12 13 14 15 /DCI/ 20 19 18 17 16 15 14 13 12 11 10 9 8 7 6 5 4 3 2 1

Prologue

My older sister, Paige, has always been a fashion freak. When we were little, she actually forced me to play Barbies with her. Of course, she'd get mad when I'd transform my doll into "Adventure Barbie." My scrappy doll with her messy hair liked to jump out of burning buildings, rescue lost dogs, and do bareback tricks on my model horse, Prancer. But like most girls, Paige only wanted to dress her flawless every-hair-in-place blonde Barbie in one outfit after the next as she played "style show." I should've known Paige might attempt to turn her fashion fetish into a career someday, but who knew it would happen so soon? Or that she would drag me along for the ride?

It all started out innocently enough when our mom (who is also a producer for Channel Five News) invited Paige and me to do some live coverage of the reopening of Wonderland, a theme park in southern California. And since Mom has involved us in a number of these "kid-oriented" gigs, it didn't seem like such a big deal. Or so I thought.

Chapter
1

"Here we are at wonderful Wonderland."
Paige doesn't even blink as she flashes a bright smile at the
camera crew before launching into a clever monologue about
the local theme park and its recent improvements. I'm sure
I'm one of the few present who knows her real opinion on
this mediocre park. "This is so last century," she told our mom
earlier today. But now she is all sunshine as she espouses the
park's many "wonders."

Meanwhile, a small crowd gathers around her, looking on
with interest like she's a celebrity. They're chatting amongst
themselves and nodding toward her like they're trying to figure out just who she is. But the problem is she's *not anybody*.
Well, she's my sister. And, in her own eyes, she's a soon-to-be-
discovered star. But then who isn't down here in La La Land,
CA, where it seems half the girls I know have a bad case of
celebrity-itis? They either want to be famous themselves or
connected to someone who already is famous.

I would never admit this to Paige, but she's got the look
of a star. Not to mention the attitude. Plus, she knows how

to dress. And it doesn't hurt that she's got peaches and cream skin, straight white teeth, clear blue eyes, and nearly natural blonde hair that despite being long always looks perfect. Not unlike her old Barbie doll. Some people have compared Paige's looks to Cameron Diaz, but in all fairness, Paige might even be prettier. Not that you'll hear those words coming from my mouth anytime soon. And certainly not while Paige is within hearing distance. I love my sister, but that girl's head is big enough already.

Anyway, as usual, I am hiding behind my video camera, acting as if I'm a member the Channel Five camera crew, although I'm fully aware that this is live coverage and my shots will not be used. Still, it's good practice as well as my best excuse to remain behind the scenes—or in other words, *in my comfort zone*. Not only that, but my camera helps to cover the conspicuous pimple that's threatening to erupt on my forehead today. Okay, so I am a little self-conscious and a bit insecure when it comes to my looks. But who wouldn't be with someone like Paige for a sister?

As I zoom in on Paige's picture-perfect face, I notice that the wind has blown a silky strand of hair across her highly glossed lips, and it sticks there like a fly on flypaper. She casually peels the strand off and continues to rattle on about the park's new and improved amenities, like it's no big deal.

"It's the twenty-fifth anniversary here at Wonderland." She addresses the camera. "And crowds have gathered here today to celebrate the reopening of the recently renovated theme park. More than two million dollars were spent bringing the park back to its former glory and, as you can see, everything looks clean and new and idyllic."

I try not to be overly wowed with my sister's natural gift

for gab, but sometimes the girl totally floors me. How does she do it? Still, I never let on that I'm impressed. By the same token, I never let on that I'm intimidated. Not even by her looks. It's not that I'm a dog. My friends all assure me that I'm relatively attractive. But, hey, they're my friends. What else are they going to say?

The cameras continue to roll and Paige rambles on, and she's starting to get this look in her eye, almost like she's become bored with her subject matter. Not that I blame her. I mean, there's only so much you can say about a second-rate theme park, no matter how much money they throw at it.

Fortunately for Paige, my mom is signaling for her to wrap it up by slashing her hand across her throat and mouthing "cut." And Paige, used to this routine, makes her graceful exit. "And now back to the anchor desk at Channel Five News."

"That was good," Mom tells her, but her eyes are on the monitor and I can tell by her expression that she's listening to her headset, probably taking direction from someone back at the station. She nods and says, "Okay. Sure, no problem, we can do that." Then she turns back to the camera crew. "They want us to get a few more minutes of airtime—they decided to cut the trucker story. So we'll be back on in fifteen. Everybody hang tight."

"What more can I say about Wonderland?" Paige demands, letting out a sigh that sounds like she just ran a five-minute mile. Sometimes my sister can be a real prima donna.

"I don't know," Mom says absently. She's still listening to her headset as if there's another big story she should be going after. "Just ad lib, okay?"

"How about if we go shoot near the entrance," suggests Sam Holliday. Sam's the head cameraman and a very nice guy, as well as the first person to let me handle a real camera.

Mom nods. "Good idea. Maybe we can get some of the park's guests to say a few words and give Paige a break." Now Mom points to me. "Or perhaps Erin can take a turn being on camera."

This is all it takes to make my sister stand up and take notice. And I know her well enough to see that she is not ready to share the limelight with anyone—especially me. And this, I must admit, is a relief.

"I'll interview some guests." Paige takes the second mic and we head over to the entrance area. We're barely set up when Mom gives Paige the signal to start. Then Mom heads off to use her cell phone.

"Here we are again for the big reopening of Wonderland," Paige says with another brilliant smile. "As you can see the people are *pouring* into the theme park this afternoon." An overstatement since there are about six people trickling in at the moment. "And here's a fresh idea—since the Golden Globes are next month, let's pretend like this is the red carpet and we are on *fashion watch*."

Then with mic in hand, Paige approaches a couple of unsuspecting teenage girls. They look a bit wary as to whether they want to be on TV or not, but my sister quickly disarms them by smiling and saying, "Welcome to Wonderland, girls. Is this your first time here?"

One girl nods without speaking, but the other girl is a little braver. "Yeah. We decided to come since it was half price today."

"And did you get those Capri pants for half price as well?" asks Paige. Well, I almost drop my camera, except that I'm curious to record the girl's reaction and I have to admit the baggy, white cropped pants were a bad choice. Not only do they make her butt look big, but there's a spill stain on one knee.

The girl looks shocked, but her friend just nudges her with an elbow, then giggles. "Yeah," the friend tells Paige, "she *did* get them on sale. How'd you know that?"

Paige smiles slyly. "Oh, it's a gift. So how would you describe your fashion style today?" she asks the half-price girl who seems to be speechless. "Campy casual or theme park comfort or thrift shop chic?"

"Uh, I guess it's theme park comfort," the girl mutters.

"Well, comfort *is* important," says Paige, turning to the other girl. "And how about you?" she asks. The girl frowns down at her black T-shirt. It's well worn with a faded white skull on the front. "Sort of revisited Goth perhaps?"

I wince inwardly but keep my camera focused and running. In a twisted way this is actually kind of good.

The girl shrugs. "Yeah . . . it's an old shirt."

"And it's just *adorable* on you," says Paige, "and it reminds me of the good old days." She's smiling back at the camera now and totally ignoring our mom, who is off the phone now, but freaking out as she sends all kinds of throat slashing "cut-cut-cut" signals Paige's direction, although no one is paying attention. I actually think the camera crew is enjoying Paige's little spectacle—or else they're too shocked to shut it down.

"And I'll be the first one to admit that fashion is subjective," Paige continues. "After all, this is only a theme park. But on the other hand, you just never know who you might bump into." She laughs then turns back to the camera. "As you can all see everyone is having a fabulous time at Wonderland today. They've put on their very best togs and are parading about for the world to enjoy."

Then Paige continues to describe outfits, turning what was supposed to be theme park coverage into a great big *What Not to Wear* spot. And by the time the camera crew finally does shut down after five long minutes of Paige's merciless attacks, Mom's face is getting those weird red blotches — not a good sign.

"Paige Forrester!" Mom seethes. "What on earth do you think you were doing?"

"Ad libbing," Paige says lightly.

Sam chuckles as he pats Mom on the back. "Don't worry, Brynn," he tells her, "who really watches the five o'clock news anyway?"

Mom turns and actually glares at him now. "Well, have no doubts that this piece will be cut out of the six o—" But she cuts herself off to listen to her headset again. Now she's grimacing as if someone back at the station is speaking way too loudly. Make that yelling, because I can hear him fairly well and it sounds a lot like her boss, Max. And the words he's using would not be acceptable on the air.

"You probably got Mom fired," I whisper to Paige.

Her brows crease slightly. "No, you don't really think—"

"I didn't *put* her up to anything," Mom says loudly. "Listen, Max, I—" But she's interrupted again and we can all hear him shouting.

I fold my camera closed and shake my head at Paige. "See what you did?"

Paige nods without speaking and her eyes look worried. For some reason this makes me feel a tiny bit better about my sister's sensibility, or rather lack of it. Still, I'm wondering what we would really do if Mom lost her job. It's only been three years since Dad died and our world was turned upside down. Since that time, Mom has worked long and hard to gain respect at the station—enough respect to land her this producing job about six months ago. And despite her hard work, there are still some Channel Five employees who think she got her promotion out of pity ... simply because her husband (our dad), Dan Forrester, the beloved anchor on the Channel Five news for more than a decade, had been tragically killed in a plane wreck. To think that Paige could've messed this all up in just a few minutes is seriously disturbing.

Chapter
2

"*Do you have any idea what kind of a position* you've placed me in?" Mom asks Paige as we're leaving the theme park.

"I was just joking around, Mom." Paige is using her "little girl" voice now—it used to work on our dad, but Mom's a lot savvier.

"You do not joke around with the news."

"But I remember Dad used to joke—"

"Your father earned the right to make a few well-timed and lighthearted comments." Mom's voice is growing sharper. "Not that he would have abused that right by treating people the way you did just now, Paige Marie."

We've reached our vehicles and the guys are quietly loading their equipment into the news van, probably trying to lay low as Mom and Paige continue their public family squabble. Good thing the cameras aren't rolling now.

"I trusted you to act professionally, Paige." Mom's voice remains angry. "And you let me down. You have actually placed my job in jeopardy. Do you understand that?"

"I'm sorry." Paige actually looks like she's on the verge of real tears now. Suddenly I wish there was something I could say to smooth this thing over — for everyone.

"I'm glad you're sorry," Mom continues. "But that doesn't change a thing. I'm on my way to talk to Max now. I can only imagine the calls he must be getting. He even said that some of your *fashion victims* might try to sue the station. Did you ever consider that?"

Paige is crying now. "I'm sorry, Mom," she chokes out. "I'm really, really sorry."

"Maybe it won't be such a big deal," I say cautiously to Mom. "I mean, I've heard that bad publicity is better than no publicity."

Mom looks at me like I have rocks in my head, but after a moment, she reluctantly smiles. "You could be right, Erin. At least the viewers will have something to talk about."

"I don't *ever* want to be in front of a camera again," Paige declares.

"Oh, don't be so melodramatic." Mom reaches over and hugs Paige. "Hopefully this will all blow over by tomorrow."

"I'm sorry, Mom." Paige sniffs, wiping her damp cheeks with her hands.

Mom pulls out a tissue and gives it to her. "And I'm sorry I made you cry."

"And I'm going to pray that something good comes out of this," I say quietly. Being the only believer in the family, it's awkward talking about my faith, but I want to keep trying. As usual, Mom and Paige give me a tolerant but slightly skeptical look ... like they wonder what planet I just arrived from.

As we say good-bye to Mom, wishing her luck at the mad Max meeting, and begin to head home, I do pray. Silently.

Driving north on the freeway, I pray that God will make something good come out of Paige's fiasco. I know that her debacle might be considered "small stuff," but I think God cares. And I don't want Mom to lose her job.

Other than a few sniffs, Paige is silent too. It isn't until I exit into Pasadena that she finally speaks.

"Do you really think Mom could get fired over this?"

"I don't know . . ."

"We'd probably have to quit school and get jobs."

Like quitting school would be a sacrifice for Paige. She's supposedly a sophomore at PCC (Pasadena City College), but as usual, she doesn't take her education too seriously. And although I'm only a freshman at UCLA's School of Theater, Film, and Television, I'll bet that I can catch up with her as far as credits go by the end of the year. Of course, competitiveness is just one of the hazards of being "Irish twins." Not that we're really Irish or twins. But that's what they call siblings who are born within a year of each other—and Paige is only eleven months older than me. So yeah . . . we're competitive.

But where Paige intimidates me in the beauty department, I overshadow her in the brains department. Most of the time—not always—it seems a fair trade. And this is one of those times when I could use my wit to knock her down a peg or two. But I guess she's suffered enough for the day. Besides, I remind myself, that's not how Jesus would treat her. I'm just trying to think of something comforting to tell her when the next thing I know she's on her phone. And it figures; she's called Addison Leiberman—the guy who plays Clinton to her Stacy.

It's not that I don't like Addison (although I'm not terribly fond of him) but it's so predictable that Paige would call him in her "hour of need." Usually, despite the fact that he and she are fashion freaks and he worships her, she's too busy to give him the time of day. Until she needs something. And right now it's consolation she's seeking as she pours out her "poor me" story.

"I was just trying to spice things up," she says finally. "I don't see why it turned into such a big deal. Seriously, some people get paid to do what I did. What about Stacy London and Clinton Kelly? No one ever picks on them. And Joan Rivers and Melissa?" she pauses to listen. "I know!" she declares triumphantly. "And Steven Cojocaru has been known to tear people to shreds. Well, no, Mr. Blackwell died a few years ago." And on and on she blathers about fashion and critics and how people shouldn't be so sensitive, until I'm forced to tune her out.

By the time we get home, Paige's courage has been fully restored and she's even agreeing to go out with Addison, which is something she'd sworn off a few weeks ago. And it actually sounds as if the two of them are making a plan to — big surprise here — critique other people's fashion sense! I would attempt to dissuade my shallow sister but I have a feeling it would be futile.

"Addison is going to call in to the station," Paige tells me as we walk toward our condo. We used to have a real house ... back before Dad died and the economy went south. But the condo's okay. It has a good pool and maintenance people to do the yard work. "He's going to pretend he's a viewer." She giggles as she unlocks the front door of our two-story unit. "And he promised to go on and on about how brilliant that segment was and how great I did and how he wishes they'd do something like that on regular basis."

"You're kidding?" I frown as I retrieve my camera, then toss my backpack onto the bench in the foyer. "Did he even see it?"

"Of course not. Why would he?"

"So he's lying."

"I just told him all about it, Erin. You heard me."

"Yeah, but you told him your version. What about the people you trashed on live TV? Do you wonder how they felt?"

"They should thank me for my honest expertise." She opens her phone again, setting her pale pink Kate Spade bag on the breakfast bar. She recently picked the purse up on eBay for "next to nothing," or so she says. "I was simply doing a fashion intervention. Who knows how this might help them in the future?"

As she checks her phone for messages, I retreat to my room. And I'm asking myself how it's possible that some people can be so dense sometimes—not to mention flaky. I mean, one moment she's tearing them to shreds and the next moment she's "helping" them. And one minute she feels remorse for her unscripted diversion and the next she thinks it was perfectly warranted. I just don't get it.

As I turn on my computer, Paige bursts in.

"I can't believe it!" she shrieks.

"What?" My heart's racing and suddenly I'm afraid something has happened to Mom. My greatest fear since losing Dad is that we'll lose Mom too. Then it will be just Paige and me. And that is very, very scary.

"I have a bunch of texts and voicemail messages."

"Huh?"

"Friends who are telling me that I was great on the news."

"Oh ..." I feel a weird mixture of relief and dismay.

"Isn't that nice?" She smiles brightly.

"Yeah, sure." I turn away from her and restrain myself from growling.

She giggles as she exits. "Hey, this last one is from Mollie Tyson and she's saying that I rock!"

Now this makes me mad, but I'm determined not to show it. Mollie is *my* best friend and has been since seventh grade. I don't get why she's suddenly encouraging Paige like this. Well, except for the fact that Mollie thinks Paige is the coolest thing since iced mocha. And while I can forgive Mollie for being starstruck and a little superficial, since she's always been a little like that, it's hard to believe she'd condone what Paige just did. After all, Mollie is a Christian and she knows we're supposed to love our neighbors and be kind to each other. But I try not to think about this as I start to download some recent photos into my computer. I mean, really, I shouldn't judge Mollie. Maybe she's just trying to be nice to Paige. And yet … it just doesn't seem right. Since Mollie is my friend, I decide it's okay for me to give her a piece of my mind. She has to forgive me if I step on her toes, right?

Feeling more than a little irked, I hit my speed dial and suddenly she's on the other end. "Mollie!" I jump right in. "Why on earth are you texting Paige that *she rocks*? Didn't you see those poor girls she embarrassed at Wonderland?"

"I thought it was funny."

"But they were publicly humiliated. How would you like to be in their shoes?"

"But what Paige said was true. They did need some fashion help."

"But it seemed so mean spirited."

There's a quiet lull and I almost think she hung up on me. Maybe I came on a little strong.

"Yeah . . ." she mutters quietly. "I guess it was a little mean."

I feel a bit relieved. "And the worst part is that my mom's in trouble now."

"Seriously?"

"Her boss was furious. She could lose her job."

"Oh . . . I'm sorry. I didn't even think about that."

"And Paige is acting like it's no big deal. Like she thinks she's Mother Teresa to the fashion-impoverished population of the planet."

Mollie laughs.

"I wasn't really trying to be funny." I let out a loud sigh of frustration.

"Sometimes you just can't help yourself, Erin. And, really, you shouldn't take it too seriously."

"And if my mom loses her job and I have to quit school and go to work just to help pay the bills?"

"Oh . . . well . . . that probably won't happen. Besides, re-member what Jesus said."

"Huh?"

"Don't worry about tomorrow—it'll take care of itself."

Now I do feel a little silly because I really want to live my life like I believe this, but sometimes it's so hard. "Yeah . . . I suppose you're right."

"So . . . speaking of not worrying," she continues, "how did you do on your finals this week?"

I flop down onto my bed and close my eyes. "Okay, I guess."

"Man, I wish I could say the same."

"I'm sure you did fine."

"Hey, I almost forgot to tell you. I got a callback on the commercial job—the one for that new protein bar."

"That's great. Way to go!"

"Yeah, my next audition is on Monday. I wonder if they want me to look fat or thin. I mean, I can do both." She giggles. Mollie is kind of short and curvy and her dream is to have a successful acting career, and so far she seems to be off to a fairly good start. She had the lead in most of our high school plays, she's had some bit parts and commercials, and her portfolio is slowly growing. She says it's an uphill battle when you don't look like Julia Roberts. But I think her wavy red hair and sea green eyes give her a unique look. Plus her voice has this really interesting throaty quality that seems to get people's attention. I've encouraged her to go for it because I tend to think God wants us to follow our dreams.

"I'm sure you'll be great whichever way they go."

"I know, but I just hope I'm not playing the fat girl."

"Maybe you'll do both. The before and after girl. You know they do digital adjustments." I sit up in bed, looking at my slightly bedraggled reflection in the dresser mirror. Sometimes I think I could use some digital adjusting too.

"I know ... but it kind of feels like cheating."

"Well, in the old days they said the camera never lied. Nowadays you never know what kind of enhanced images you're looking at." I stand in front of my mirror now, taking a good hard look at myself. Straggly dark brown hair, green eyes, straight nose, small mouth ... I wonder what I'd do to enhance this. For sure I'd erase that zit starting to show on my forehead.

"And that is exactly why some girls—like me—have self-image problems, Erin."

"Hey, you're not the only one. I simply figure that by now every girl has to know that when she's looking at any media image, it's probably an illusion."

"But sometimes I wish it could all go back to reality."

"Yeah. I know what you mean. But I have to admit that I don't mind tweaking on my own nature photos a little. Not to make the birds prettier or the whales skinnier . . . just to make the general photo more appealing with light and hue and clarity." I turn sideways now, checking out my figure, which is okay in a short, compact way, but nothing like Paige's long waist and perfect curves. And suddenly I feel silly for being so self-absorbed. I'm glad Mollie can't see me.

"I can't believe we have three blessed weeks off from school," she says. "I'm so in need of some sleep. So what are your plans for winter break?"

"First of all to chill a little. I've had a pretty heavy class load too. But I also want to get out to the desert."

"The desert?" Mollie sounds appalled. "What for?"

"Photos. I want to do the Mojave and maybe even down to Baja if the weather cooperates."

"What can you shoot down there? I mean, besides cactuses or cacti or whatever they call them."

"There are some amazing birds and plants, and even the gray whales." I consider asking her to join me, but I can already guess her response. Mollie isn't exactly a nature girl. Her idea of the great outdoors is more like a beach, preferably one in Balboa or Laguna. Throw in a cabana and a fruity drink with an umbrella and she's in heaven. For more serious adventurous treks I usually rely on my buddy and fellow camera buff, Lionel Stevens. But I know he's joining his family in Tahoe during winter break so I might be on my own. Although I wonder whether Mom will approve of me heading south of the border all by myself in my good old Jeep Wrangler.

"Hey," I tell Mollie as I hear a beep, "I have another call coming in and I wonder if it's Mom. I better go."

"Later."

It turns out to be Mom and thankfully she sounds a little less stressed than earlier. "Is Paige home?" she asks me. "I've tried to call her, but I go straight to voicemail."

"She's gabbing with her fans." I say, perhaps a bit too sarcastically.

"Fans?"

"Yeah. Apparently all her friends think she's a star and that she was great on the news tonight. And that should make you feel a little better."

"That's actually why I'm calling, Erin. Could you go get her and put her on, please?"

"Sure." I go back out into the great room where Paige is still on her phone, but now she has the TV turned on as well, although it's muted. But she's watching her favorite reality channel and what appears to be a rerun of *The OC*. "Mom wants to talk to you," I tell her with a warning look.

"Oh?" She frowns. "Sorry, Kelsey, I have to go. Yeah, thanks!" She closes her phone and peers at me. "Is she still mad?"

I act dumb and just hand her my phone.

"Hi, Mom," she says cautiously. Then she just listens ... and listens ... and finally her face begins to brighten. "Really?"

Okay, now I'm curious. What's going on and why can't I hear? After all, it's my phone. I lean my head closer to Paige and try to eavesdrop, barely hearing my mom's voice as she says, "It's all pretty speculative. But the plan is that tomorrow we'll meet with Helen and, well, we'll just see what happens."

"Helen Hudson?" Paige's voice is high pitched. "I'm really going to—"

"Don't get your hopes up," Mom warns. "Like I said, it's very speculative. Chances are it will go nowhere. But at least it's smoothed over Max's ruffled feathers."

"This is so exciting!"

"And tell Erin I want her to come too."

"What for?" Paige gives me a curious look then pushes me away so I can't hear the rest of the conversation.

"Bye, Mom!" Paige says happily after another minute. She hands me back the phone. "Did you hear that?" Her eyes are bright with excitement.

"Part of it. Who is Helen Hudson?"

"Just one of the best producers of reality TV."

"Oh?"

"And she wants to meet me!"

"So I heard."

"Do you know how exciting this is?"

I shrug.

"This could be my big break, Erin. If Helen really likes me, she might want to do some kind of show."

"What kind of show?"

"I don't know. Maybe like *What Not to Wear*."

"But you're just a kid."

She stands straighter, giving me an indignant look. "FYI. I'm nearly twenty. And lots of people younger than me have made it. Ever hear of Lindsay Lohan or the Olsen Twins?"

I roll my eyes.

"Jessica Alba? Amanda Bynes?"

I hold up my hands. "Yes, of course. Stop with the list."

"So why not just be happy for me? Maybe this is my big chance."

"Well, I'm just relieved that Mom's not in trouble."

Paige sighed. "Yeah, me too."

"And, yeah, I think it's cool for you, Paige."

"Maybe for you too?"

"Why?"

"Apparently Sam caught you filming me and it showed up in the segment. Mom said that Helen asked who the other girl was, and when she told her it was you, Helen asked to see *both* of the Forrester sisters. The appointment's at one tomorrow." Now Paige is dancing around the great room like a maniac. "This is so great! So great!"

But I'm not convinced. I have no idea why I need to be included in this "speculative" meeting. And I'm not sure that I even want to go. However, it doesn't seem like I have a choice. Most of all I'm relieved that Mom is off the hook—or so it seems. For her sake, I'll be cooperative tomorrow. Whatever this is, I'm guessing it'll all blow over anyway. At least in regard to me. Maybe Paige is right; maybe this will be her big break. For her sake, I hope that's how it goes down. I just don't see any good reason for me to be involved.

Chapter

3

Paige has literally changed her outfit about seventeen times today. Her room looks like a garage sale and we need to head out of here in about ten minutes.

"Be honest," she tells me. When am I not? "Does this look good?" She does a 360 without even tripping over the shoes and bags and clothes and things that are strewn across her floor.

I pretend to scrutinize her outfit — which honestly doesn't seem much different than the last one — after she decided to go more "classic and timeless" in lieu of "trendy and faddish." She has on a neat gray skirt topped with a fitted pale pink jacket. "It's BCBG," she tells me like I get it.

"It looks fine." I simply nod then glance at my watch as in *hint-hint*. "And the other sixteen outfits looked good too."

"But is it *have-your-own-TV-show* good?"

"Who says you're going to have your own show?"

She gives me her *duh* look. "That's why Helen Hudson wants to see me, Erin."

"You don't know that for sure."

"I already told you. *Helen Hudson produces reality shows.* She's big. She's hot. And she wouldn't waste her time meeting with me if she didn't have a serious idea for a new show . . . Unless she wants to cast me into one of her other reality shows?" Paige has a dreamy look now.

"Or maybe she wants to cast you as a script girl," I suggest.

Paige's brow creases. "Well . . . then I would consider it. And then I would work my way up."

"Why don't you work your way out of your room and into my car," Mom calls at Paige from the front door. "Come on, we need to go."

Paige shoves her feet into her favorite black pumps, which have the same BCBG initials as her jacket. Then she hurries to grab up a selection of accessories, including belts, jewelry, and scarves, which she stuffs into an oversized bag. Then she gets her pale pink purse and we're on our way.

As usual, I feel a little dowdy next to my stylish sister. And that's *after* she forced me to "clean up my act and dress decently." Even so, the only designer I'm wearing is from Target—Isaac something-or-other. That's how much I'm into haute fashion. And the main reasons I bought this simple chocolate-brown jacket are that 1) it fit me pretty well, 2) I liked it, and 3) it was on sale. As for my A-line print skirt, which I used to like when I occasionally wore skirts, it's simply a piece I picked up at my favorite retro store last year. And my tan suede boots? Well, I've had them for several years and although they're a little worn, they're also very comfortable. Paige had been unimpressed with my "improvements" but was so focused on her own appearance that she let it go.

But by the time we're walking into the sleek-looking studio offices—all glass, dark wood, and stainless steel—I feel like a little brown mouse next to Paige. And have I mentioned that she doesn't really *walk*? No, Paige kind of struts like she thinks she's on a Parisian runway, and yet she makes it look almost natural, which I find extremely aggravating. If I attempted to walk like that I would either look like an idiot or fall flat on my face. So I don't.

But I feel even more out of place when we stand in front of the girl at the desk. Or maybe we've just arrived on a different planet because she looks a little strange. She's in black from head to toe, but it's her hair and makeup that capture my attention. Her glossy, straight black hair is cut in a sharp triangular shape. Her face is so white she's slightly vampire-like. Although her eyes are dramatically outlined in black, her lips are so pale that they almost don't seem to be there at all. I wonder if she's got her own aspirations for a TV show too. Horror perhaps? Or maybe sci-fi. Yes, I can definitely see her as an alien.

"We're here to see Ms. Hudson," my mom tells her.

"Your name, please?"

"I'm Paige Forrester," Paige answers coolly, as if her name might be recognizable.

"And I'm Brynn Forrester," my mom offers. "From Channel Five News."

I don't bother to introduce myself. I'm pretty sure Sci-fi Girl doesn't care. She just nods in a bored way. "Go ahead and sit down. I'll let her know you're here." But then she returns to her computer screen and I can tell by her expression she's much more interested in that than she is in us. Maybe the mother ship is calling. So we sit and wait. And we wait and wait. And finally a whole hour has passed and I'm ready to make a run for it.

"Helen Hudson doesn't seem all that interested in seeing us," I point out as I check my watch again. "Do you guys mind if I take off?"

"She's probably tied up with something." Mom's voice sounds patient, but I can tell she's getting irritated too. "Let's give her a little more time."

I try not to groan as I lean back into the hard and sticky vinyl chair. It's a weird shape that sort of goes with Sci-fi Girl's hair. You'd think they'd offer more comfortable furniture if they make people wait this long.

"I could probably take this appointment by myself," Paige says, "if you two get tired of waiting."

Mom clears her throat. "No ... I think I'd rather stick around."

Just then a tall woman with extremely short white hair emerges from behind the closed door. She's wearing a bright-colored scarf that seems to be tangled in the armload of papers she carrying. "Here, Sabrina." She dumps the mess onto Sci-fi Girl's desk. "Make three sets of copies. File one. FedEx the others." Then the woman straightens out her scarf and turns to us. "You must be the Forresters. Please forgive me for keeping you waiting. I'm sure you understand how little crises can derail a schedule."

Mom stands and smiles, quickly introducing each of us, but it seems that Helen Hudson is fully aware of our identity as she ushers us into her office, which thankfully has more-comfortable furniture to sit in.

"Tell me about yourself." She directs this to Paige while leaning back in her chair with her hands folded in front of her. She studies my sister, like a lion might watch its prey before pouncing. Paige seems oblivious as she begins to chatter away.

And I suppress the urge to yawn since this kind of monologue is way too familiar to me. Paige goes into great detail about her interest in fashion and popular culture and film and television and yada-yada-blah-blah-blah.

But what holds my attention is how intently Helen Hudson seems to be listening—and yet it's as if she's somewhere else too. Her brow creases and I feel as if I can see the wheel mechanisms turning around in her head. Although I have no idea about what she's thinking.

"Yes, yes," she says quickly, actually cutting my sister off in mid-sentence. "Now answer a few questions for me, Paige Forrester."

"Sure." Paige recrosses her long, slender legs, sits up a bit straighter, flashes another bright smile, and waits.

Helen smiles back, almost in a catty way. "So tell me, Paige, are you much into partying?" Her brows arch in a knowing way.

Paige looks slightly stumped as she shrugs, glancing at Mom and me as if we can help. "How do you mean exactly?"

The room is quiet now and I'm having flashbacks to a couple of years ago when Paige and her friends were running wild, drinking and staying out late even on school nights. Then Paige's grades dropped, and my mom put her foot down and grounded Paige until she graduated. It wasn't exactly a happy era in our house, but I was relieved to see Mom acting like a parent.

"Oh, I'm sure you know what I'm talking about." Helen leans forward, studying Paige as if she's peering through a microscope. "Are you involved with a party crowd at all? Do you go clubbing? Social drinking? You know the sort of thing I mean. Friends, late nights, let the good times roll."

"Well, yes, I *know* what you mean. But, no … I'm not *really* like that. I'll admit I went through a little bit of a wild spell during my senior year in high school … after Dad died." She looks at Mom with uncertainty. "But I'm not so much into that now. It's not like I'm a hermit or a wet blanket or anything. And I do have friends who still like to party and sometimes I hang out with them, but …" She frowns with uncertainty. "Does that mean you're not interested? I mean … was this going to be some kind of *Laguna Beach* or *The Hills* or that new show, *Malibu Beach*? Because I can *act* like I'm a partier if—"

Helen Hudson laughs. "No, no, that's not what I'm going for. Not at all. You see, this is a show I began to put together last summer. And I had a popular celebrity lined up—I won't mention her name—but she got arrested for driving under the influence and she's only seventeen. It pretty much put the brakes on the project. By the way, how old are you?"

"Nineteen. Nineteen and a half."

"So you're still a teen, and I'm sure teen girls would relate to you."

"Oh, yeah," Paige says with confidence, "I'm sure they would."

"So I can see this is worth a shot."

Paige is beaming. "A shot?"

"Yes. I'd like to do a screen test with you first. Then we'll revise the package and do another pitch and—" She waves her hands as she interrupts herself. "Never mind about that now." She puts on a pair of purple-rimmed glasses and begins writing something down on paper.

Paige elbows me and I can tell by her expression she's just bursting to talk, but she's exercising self-control.

"What sort of show are you planning?" our mom ventures.

Helen looks up blankly. "Oh, I thought I told you."

"No, not really."

"Oh, well, if the screen test delivers and if we come to an agreement, and if the revised pitch is received how I expect it will be—because we've already got sponsors lined up and the network was onboard—Anyway, if all goes well, Paige will be hosting a reality show that's targeted at a teen audience. The focus will be fashion, of course, and it will all be shot on location . . . so some travel will be involved. I thought the concept might need a big name to launch it, but more recently I decided that if I could find just the right girl, and if I knew that she was stable and mature and with no juvenile record, we could move forward." She glances at Mom. "Trust me, I already checked on this or I wouldn't be wasting my time now. You'd be surprised how many young people already have police records."

Paige laughs nervously.

"My hope was that we could launch the girl right along with the show. It's not that hard really—not if the ingredients are right. And when I saw Paige on the news last night, I thought, 'There's my girl.'" She studies Paige again. "I'm feeling very hopeful."

Okay, I'm sitting here feeling practically invisible, not to mention totally unnecessary. Like, what a waste of my time. Why did I have to get dragged in here for this? Sure, my sister is pretty and talented and all that stuff, but why torture me like this? Then, as if reading my thoughts, Helen turns to me. "And you probably wonder why you're here . . . Erin, is it?"

"Yeah." I force a wimpy smile.

"Well, I saw you in the background with your camera and I thought how natural you two girls looked together.

And when I heard you were sisters, I thought, 'Ah-hah—that might just work.'"

"Work?" I give her an uncertain look.

"Yes, I think Paige could use a sidekick."

"Well, she's gotten a few kicks in," I confess.

Helen laughs. "But you two do get along, don't you? Your mother said you did."

"Of course," Paige assures her. "We're actually pretty good friends."

"Well, most of the time," I admit. "But when we're not, you don't want to be around to hear it."

Helen winks at me. "I like your honesty, Erin."

"To be totally honest," I continue, "I'm not that comfortable in front of the camera. I mean, I'm flattered you'd consider me. But I'm really more of a behind-the-scenes girl."

Helen frowns. "Seriously? Are you saying you wouldn't want to be a star, Erin?"

I shrug. "Not really."

"I find that hard to believe."

"Well, how about you?" I challenge her. "Do you like being in the limelight with a camera pointing at you?"

Helen smiles, then nods in an understanding way. "I see your point."

I relax a little.

"You mentioned travel would be involved," Mom says now.

"Yes. I'm thinking of the fashion world at large. New York, Milan, Tokyo, London, Paris ..." Helen waves her hands. "I see this show as being a form of enrichment. Because I, for one, am getting a bit weary of some of the senseless shows that teens are tuning into. I'm hoping that teen sleaze has seen its day. I want this to be a show that teaches as much as it entertains. I know that teens are interested in fashion and I'm hoping this show will expose them to something beyond some of the common trash they're watching on MTV." She makes a dramatic pause, looking directly at my sister. "Paige will cover fashion events wherever they're occurring. She'll offer her opinions as well as advice and tips about style, and she'll do interviews with models, designers, and anyone linked with the fashion world. She'll basically generate enthusiasm toward style and fashion. The show will be called *On the Runway*. Perhaps it will be *On the Runway with Paige Forrester.* Something to that effect."

"That all sounds good . . . in theory." Mom's voice has that edge of hesitation in it. "But I'm a little concerned about that kind of travel. Paige is only nineteen and—"

"Nineteen and a half," Paige reminds her. "And I think the travel sounds delicious. I think the whole concept is absolutely brilliant." Paige's blue eyes, normally bright, now glitter with excitement and her smile is so wide I think her cheeks must be aching. But she sits perfectly, legs neatly crossed, hands folded in her lap; the quintessential lady.

"Thank you." Helen turns her attention back to Mom. "The show will need a producer," she tells her. "Perhaps you'd be interested. That way you could keep an eye on her."

I can feel Paige slumping ever so slightly, not that anyone would notice, but I can tell some of the wind just got sucked out of her sails. She is not into having Mom along as her chaperone. I actually think it's pretty funny.

"I appreciate the thought," Mom says quickly. "But I'm sure you can't guarantee how long a show like this will run— if it makes it at all. And because I'm the sole supporter of our household, I feel I need to stick with Channel Five."

"I totally understand."

Mom glances at me. "But I do like your idea of including Erin in—"

"*Mom!*" I give her a warning look.

"I'm sorry, Erin, but I think you and your sister would be a good team."

"But I—"

"And I have an idea," Mom continues as if I'm not even in the room. "Erin is actually quite good with the camera. And I understand her desire to stay on the sidelines—she probably gets that kind of shyness from me. But how about including her in the show as part of the camera crew."

Helen slowly nods. "You know, that's not a bad idea. One sister in front of the camera, one sister behind it." She peers at me again. "But how would you feel about being filmed while you are filming? Not all the time, of course, but occasionally."

I don't even know what to say. Mostly I'd like to make a fast break for the door.

"Well, we don't have to resolve everything today," Helen says. "Here." She gives Paige a small card. "You give these guys a call and they'll set up your screen test. And I'll be in touch with you next week." She stands now, as if cueing us that this interview is over.

Paige smiles so big that I wonder if her cheeks ever get tired. Then she reaches out and shakes Helen's hand, warmly thanking her, and then Helen ushers us out and tells us to have a good weekend and that she'll be in touch. We're barely outside of the building when Paige lets out a loud whoop. "I can't believe it!" she squeals, "I *cannot* believe it!"

"Don't start celebrating just yet," Mom warns her. "There are still some bridges to cross first."

But Paige looks like she's walking—make that strutting—on air as we head for the car. On the other hand, my feet feel like lead weights as I try to figure a graceful exit out of what's sure to turn into a catastrophe, for me anyway. Because, for the life of me, I can't see how I would possibly enjoy being involved in a show like this. It's like being forced to play Barbies again. And wouldn't this mean I'd have to give up film school? As much as I'd hate to play the spoiler, I can't agree to something like this. Hopefully the whole thing will blow over, and although I'll act as if I'm sad for Paige's sake, I'll be extremely thankful for my own.

Chapter
4

"*No way!*" *Mollie shrieks when I tell her* the news on the phone. "Paige is going to have her own show? Oh, I'm so jealous. Does she need anyone else, Erin?"

Then I explain Helen Hudson's plan to use me as camera girl. "But I don't see how I can do it, Mollie. I mean, fashion is so not me. And there's film school. Really the whole idea is ridiculous."

"Wow, your enthusiasm is underwhelming."

"Sorry," I tell her. "But I really don't want to be involved."

"Maybe I could be the camera girl," she suggests.

"You don't even know how to use the camera on your phone," I point out.

"You could give me a quick course on cameras. I'm a fast learner when I set my mind to it."

Oddly enough, Mollie's genuine interest in this project is making me reconsider. "I suppose this experience might look good on my résumé," I say hesitantly.

"*Duh.* How many eighteen-year-olds do you know who get to film a TV show? Seriously, why would you pass up this opportunity? But if you do, I still get dibs, okay? Not that I'm advising you to. Really, Erin, think about it. Why would you give up the chance to be on the camera crew? I wonder how much they'll pay you."

"But I'm afraid I'll be more like a *token* camera girl ... like a piece of the scenery. They probably just want me to look like Paige's little plain-Jane sister, something to make Paige look even more beautiful and glamorous ... as if she needs that."

"I hate it when you put yourself down like that, Erin. You're a pretty girl and you know it."

"I *know* it?" I look at my image in the mirror above my bureau dresser and make a face. My hair, which looks dull and dark and probably needs to be washed, is pulled back into a tight ponytail—not my best look. My face, void of makeup as usual, looks kind of pasty and in need of some sunshine. And that zit that had been threatening to erupt finally did, and right now it looks like a red headlight in the middle of my forehead.

"If you'd just put a little more time into your appearance—"

"What?" I say harshly. "Then I could look like Paige?"

"No. You could look like Erin ... only better."

"But that's not me, Mollie. You know that. I'm just not into that."

"You used to be," she reminds me.

I don't respond to this. I'm afraid I know where she's going. Unfortunately, I can't think of anything to say that will stop her.

"When are you going to get over him?" she asks me point-blank.

"What do you mean?" I decide to play dumb.

"Blake," she says in a flat voice. "When will you let it go?"

"I *have* let it go," I say. "That's like ancient history."

"Yeah, right."

"It is. I hardly ever think of him anymore." Even as I say this, I open my top drawer and remove a framed photo of Blake Josephson and me at senior prom. It was taken just two weeks before he broke up with me ... about eight months ago, not that I'm counting.

"I mean, it was understandable for you to go into a funk then, Erin. You guys had been together for almost two years ... I know you were hurting."

"And your point is?"

"My point is, *move on.*"

"I *have* moved on. I don't know what you're talking about." I slip the photo back into the drawer, burying it beneath a tangled mess of underwear and T-shirts.

"If you've really moved on, how come you won't go out with Lionel Stevens?"

"Lionel and I are just good friends," I point out. "And that's how I want to keep it."

"Fine. But let's talk about why you don't seem to care about your appearance anymore. Why have you let yourself go?"

"Thanks, a lot. With friends like you—"

"Come on, you know what I mean. You used to care more. Now you're just sort of, well, laid back."

"Maybe I don't want to be superficial. Maybe I happen to like the natural look."

"And that's fine, but you could do it with a little more panache."

"Sometimes I think you and I were swapped at birth, Mollie. You should be Paige's sister instead of me."

"Hey, I'm just being honest. If you can't take some constructive criticism from your best friend who—"

"Okay, Mollie. Thank you. I get it. You think I'm a slob. So does Paige." I feel both angry and hurt. "I only called you to tell you about the show, not to get lectured."

"I'm sorry." Her voice softens. "It's just that I care about you and sometimes it seems like you're still hung up on Blake. That worries me."

I take in a deep breath, shoot up a very quick prayer, and decide to get honest. "Okay . . . you might be right. I try not to think about him, but I guess I still feel hurt. I mean, we were so close. I thought he really loved me . . . and I loved him. He seemed like such a strong Christian, and I probably thought someday we'd get married."

"I know, Erin. I thought the same things about you guys—you were like the perfect couple. And I couldn't believe it when he did what he did."

What Blake *did* was cheat on me with Sonya Michaels. He claimed she had been the instigator, that she had flirted with him first, but the fact of the matter was that he went for the bait. And who could blame him? Sonya is gorgeous. But she's certainly not what you'd call a girl of faith. Not even close. And when Blake started dating her, he stopped going to youth group. I'm not sure which part of the breakup hurts the most—being dumped for a girl who's much hotter than me or seeing Blake take steps away from his faith. The whole thing hurts. And Mollie knows this.

"So . . . anyway . . . I wasn't sure if I should tell you this or not, but Tony told me that he's been talking to Blake."

Tony is Mollie's boyfriend. He's also Blake's best friend. Or rather, he used to be. Tony was so miffed at Blake that they quit talking too. Just one more sad side effect of our breakup. I guess I should be happy for Blake's sake that they're talking again. But I don't even know how to react to this. So I simply say, "Oh."

"Anyway, Tony said that Blake has been talking to Sonya about coming to the college fellowship group and there's a pretty good chance they'll come."

"Oh …" Again, I don't know what to say. I don't know whether to be encouraged or terrified of seeing Blake again. Especially when I thought I'd finally gotten over missing him.

"So I just thought you should know, Erin. Kind of a heads-up."

"Sure. I appreciate it."

"I almost wasn't going to tell you because I was worried that you might decide to skip out on it …"

The thought is already going through my mind, but I don't confess it. "Why would I do that?"

"To avoid him."

I sigh. "Don't worry, Mollie. I'm not going to let Blake and Sonya drive me away from fellowship."

"Oh, good." She sounds genuinely relieved. "So are you still picking me up at seven?"

"Sure." I force brightness into my voice.

"Great. I better go now. Tell Paige congrats on the TV show."

"It's not set in stone, you know."

"But knowing Paige it probably will be."

We say good-bye and hang up, and suddenly the realization that Blake and Sonya might possibly be at fellowship group tonight stops me in my tracks. Mollie was right—I do want to skip out on it. But I promised her that I wouldn't. And yet the idea of being in the same room with them … well, it's a little overwhelming.

"Hey, Erin." Paige sticks her head in my room without even knocking.

"What?" I snap at her.

"*Excuse* me," she says dramatically.

"Sorry. But you could at least knock."

Now she's all the way in my room and peering at me curiously. "What's wrong with you?"

"Nothing," I snap.

She folds her arms in front of her, then shakes her head. "What's going on, Erin? You look like you want to punch someone."

"Maybe I do." I press my lips together and tighten my fists.

"Why?" Her features soften. "What's up?"

I really don't want to tell her, but before I can ask her to leave, tears start filling my eyes. I really don't want to cry.

"Erin," she says gently, "tell me, what's wrong?"

And then, to my own shock, I pour out the whole story. Sure, Paige knows all about the breakup. But she didn't know how deeply it had hurt me. No one really did, except maybe Mollie. "And he and Sonya are going to fellowship tonight and I just really don't want to see him, but I promised Mollie I'd go. And I actually want to go because it's a cool group and I like it." And now I'm really crying.

Paige hugs me. "You will go, Erin. And you'll hold your head high and you'll look like a million bucks too."

I pull away from her and wipe my cheeks. "Yeah, right." I point to the mountain on my forehead. "I'll look more like a pathetic zit head."

Paige just laughs. "*Zit head*? Really?" Now we're both laughing. "Listen," Paige says, "we can totally cover that up."

"With what?" I ask. "A ski mask?"

Her mouth twists to one side as she studies me. "How about bangs?"

"Bangs?" I frown at her. "Cut my hair just to hide a zit?"

"You'd look good with bangs, Erin."

I roll my eyes.

"Seriously. Why don't you let me cut your hair?" She pushes me in front of my mirror, then pulls the bungee off my ponytail to let my hair fall down. "I'll take a little off the length and give you some bangs, and you'll love it."

"I'll love it, huh?"

"You used to let me cut your hair."

I nod as I stare at my image. I look even more pathetic now with my puffy eyes and dirty hair stringing down.

"Come on, Erin, it'll be fun. I'll do a whole makeover on you."

"I don't know …"

"Please," she pleads.

I just shrug. Really, what do I have to lose?

And so, like a lamb to the slaughter, I place myself in my sister's hands. She pulls out all the stops and I feel like I've just arrived at Spa Forrester. And to my surprise, it's not so bad. First, she applies a facial masque, including cucumbers over my eyes, and then she assigns me to soak in the tub. This is followed by an "exfoliating" shower, along with a shampoo and an "intensive hair treatment" that smells like coconut. When I'm done bathing, she sets me outside in the sunshine where she plans to cut my hair.

"I don't want you to see yourself until I'm all done, okay?" she says as she begins snipping away. I'm a little worried that she'll cut it too short, but instead of worrying, I just turn on my iPod and zone out. After the haircut she takes me to her room where she styles my hair and then starts to apply makeup.

"Please, don't make me look like a clown," I beg her. "Keep it natural, okay?"

"Trust me," she says for the umpteenth time. Then she chatters happily about how great it will be to do the TV show, which she is certain is in the bag. I don't say anything to rain on her parade. After all, she's trying to help me.

She steps back and looks at me. "Perfect."

"Can I see?"

"Not yet." She frowns. "We need to dress you first."

I feel like I'm about three years old as Paige takes shirts out of her own closet, holding them up to me as if I'm a paper doll. I'm surprised that she's willing to let me wear something of hers, but then I realize that I'm her project and it's all about the final results. Although Paige is taller than me, we wear about the same size in a lot of things, including shoes because her feet are small for her height whereas mine are a bit large.

It's getting close to six when she finally decides on the outfit, which turns out to be a cute little denim skirt — which she tells me I can keep — topped by a simple white T-shirt and her black suede jacket. I'm surprised she lets me wear this jacket, but I have to admit that it feels really nice. The leather is soft and buttery. I'm even more surprised when she lets me wear her Frye boots, since she just got them last fall. Like the jacket, they're black and are almost too tall for me, but Paige assures me they look great. I'm still not allowed to look in the mirror as she chooses accessories, finally deciding on simple hoops and a silver chain necklace.

"Hey, girls," Mom calls as she comes into the house. "Anyone home?"

"In here," Paige calls back.

Mom comes into Paige's room and blinks in surprise to see me. "Oh, Erin," she says with wide eyes.

"What?" I demand. "Do I look ridiculous?"

"No." She shakes her head. "Not at all. You look gorgeous."

"Really?"

"You haven't seen yourself?" Mom looks puzzled.

"I told her she can't see the results until the makeover is all done," Paige says as she does a final touch-up to my hair.

"Did you do this yourself, Paige?"

Paige nods proudly.

"Well, I'm impressed." Mom looks like she's about to cry.

"Okay," Paige says as she turns me around so I can look in the full-length mirror on her closet door. "Voila!"

I stare at my image in wonder. "It doesn't even look like me," I finally say.

"Yes, it does," Paige insists.

"It just shows how beautiful you really are," Mom adds.

Now Paige looks upset. "You don't like it?"

I'm still staring at the strange girl in the mirror. She looks stylish and pretty — her hair is cut just above the shoulders in a glossy bob and the bangs, which look good, totally cover her zit. "I like it," I tell Paige. "I mean, it'll take some getting used to. But you did a good job."

"Thanks!" Paige is beaming now. "You look hot, Erin."

"I'm just in shock," I say, still trying to absorb my new look.

"I'm getting my camera," Mom says suddenly.

I look at the clock by Paige's bed. "You better hurry. I need to get going."

So Mom snaps shots of me by myself, then me with Paige. Afterward, I grab my backpack and am about to leave.

"Wait!" Paige yells. "That backpack will NOT do."

I wait as she dashes back to her room, finally emerging with a small red purse. "It's a fake Fendi," she admits, "but a good one." Then she helps me transfer some things from my pack.

"Have fun," Mom tells me.

"You look fabulous!" Paige calls as I leave. "Knock 'em dead."

I almost feel like giggling as I head downstairs. And I feel something else too ... kind of hopeful. Not that I haven't been hopeful before, but I suppose I have been kind of gloomy lately. Still, I don't think that the hope I feel is tied to my appearance exactly. And it's certainly not tied to Blake. I honestly believe my makeover is like a God-inspired kind of hope. Kind of like a rainbow or a promise ... like something really good is coming my way. I get into my Jeep and realize I can't wait to see Mollie's reaction to my makeover.

Chapter
5

"What happened to you?" Mollie's jaw is literally hanging as she stares at me, then makes me turn around. "You look stunning, Erin!"

"Thanks. I'm Paige's newest makeover project."

"Man, do you think she'd do me?"

I shrug, feeling encouraged. "You can ask her if you want."

"You look awesome, Erin." She keeps staring at me as we go out to my Jeep. The sky is clouding up and I hope it doesn't rain, because I really do like how my hair turned out and the idea of getting all wet doesn't appeal to me.

"Did you do this because of Blake?" Mollie asks quietly as I drive toward the church.

"Not exactly. I *was* feeling bummed after you told me about Blake and Sonya maybe coming to fellowship group. Then Paige popped in and I'm sure she felt sorry for me. But what you said made sense, Mollie. I guess I had let myself go … and I'm sure it was because I was unhappy about Blake and other things. The weird thing is that I don't even feel that bad about him now. But it's not just because of this makeover.

It's more like something in me just clicked into place earlier today—like I suddenly believed that God has something better for me. I know I say that a lot, but today as I was coming to pick you up, I really *felt* it."

"That's so cool."

Thanks to Mom's photos and Paige's last-minute purse exchange, Mollie and I arrive "fashionably" late. Although the worship time hasn't begun, most of our friends are already here, grazing on munchies and chatting. I can't help but notice that some heads turn as we enter the room. I do my best to act oblivious, but I've barely stepped inside when I notice Blake standing with Tony. Sonya is right next to him, but she seems uncomfortable—in an attractive sort of way, of course. I always find it ironic that Sonya has a similar look to my sister—tall, blonde, stylish, and pretty. Maybe this is God's way of making me deal with any envy issues.

But instead of obsessing, I silently pray that God will help me to handle this awkward situation in a mature and civilized manner. And because it's only natural that we go talk to Tony, since he is Mollie's boyfriend and she plans on riding home with him afterward, I go ahead and lead the way toward the trio. "It's cool," I say quietly to Mollie. I can tell she's worried for my sake.

"Hey, Blake," I say in a normal tone. "Good to see you. Hi, Sonya." I smile at her as if we're old friends. "How're you doing?"

"Good." She nods. "How about you?"

"Really good." I smile and wish I could think of something else to say.

"Did you guys hear the news about Erin and Paige?" Mollie says suddenly.

"Huh?" I glance curiously at Mollie.

"The TV show."

"Oh, you mean the spot on Channel Five News," Sonya says. "I saw that. Paige was hilarious."

"No, that's not what I'm talking about," Mollie continues. "It's even bigger."

"What?" Sonya looks really interested now.

I'm stunned silent that Mollie is bringing this up.

"Paige and Erin might get their own TV show," Mollie tells them.

"Well, we don't know that for sure yet," I point out, finally able to speak. Although I have to admit I like the look I'm getting from Blake and Sonya. Kind of a mixture of shock and respect. "There's still the screen test next week. And Paige is really the one that—"

"And Erin gets to help on the camera crew as well as be in the show," Mollie rattles on. "And they'll travel all over the world covering fashion shows and doing interviews with models and designers and things. It's called *On the Runway*." Mollie beams at them and I have to keep from laughing at how my best friend sounds like she knows more about this gig than I do.

"Seriously?" Sonya looks truly wowed.

I nod. "Yeah. Helen Hudson is the producer. She's done a lot of—"

"I know who she is," Sonya says eagerly, rattling off some of the reality shows that Helen is involved in. "Wow, that's really cool. When will you know for sure?"

"Probably pretty soon," I tell her. I know it's kind of premature to talk about this, but I'm getting a little rush from Sonya's reaction. "Helen seems eager to get things going."

Then the music begins to get louder, and that's the signal that it's time to find seats. Still feeling Blake's eyes on me, I just smile and say, "See ya later," then head over to where Mollie and I usually sit.

"That was perfect," Mollie says quietly as we sit down.

"Thanks," I say.

I can feel myself holding my head higher than usual. And I think Paige would be proud of me. Then, as I sit there and participate in the worship time, I thank God for helping me to move a little beyond my old heartache. And, sure, I suppose the makeover didn't hurt either. There's still a part of me that wants to crane my neck to peer at Blake and to see what he's doing. But I resist that urge.

Instead, I watch Lionel, playing the drums with the worship team like he usually does. It feels like he's watching me back, and I wonder if it's because of my makeover. I know he considers me to be more of a casual, earthy kind of girl, not the kind who's a slave to fashion. And I know he appreciates this since he's pretty laid back too. Lionel and I are kind of alike in a lot of ways. We even ended up taking some of the same classes last term. Mollie doesn't get why we don't date, but I just think we're too much alike—more like brother and sister than boyfriend and girlfriend. Although I could be wrong.

Anyway, I'll have to assure Lionel that besides my little makeover I haven't really changed. I know that without Paige's intervention I couldn't have pulled this off. And no way will I look like this on a regular basis. Really, I'm still a blue jeans kind of girl at heart.

After the worship and teaching is free time, so I head straight for Lionel. "Hey," I say to him. "I thought you might've been gone by now. Aren't you still going to Tahoe for winter break?"

He nods, sticking his drumsticks in his back pocket. "Yeah. But I promised Travis I'd play tonight. I'll head out to-morrow." He then makes a funny smile. "What have you done to yourself, Erin?"

I just laugh. "Paige wanted to play makeover today and I complied."

"You look different."

"I know. I'll go back to my old scruffy self again."

"Why?"

Now that surprises me. "Why not?"

"Because you look good ... in an uptown sort of way, that is."

"Oh, well ... thanks ... I guess."

Now Sonya, with Blake trailing her reluctantly, comes alongside me. She wants to hear more about the TV show.

"TV show?" Lionel looks surprised, so I fill him in. I try to play it down as they all listen, but as I'm talking I can feel Blake's eyes on me. And after a few minutes, I feel like I'm in over my head and I want to escape. I mean, it's one thing to realize I've made a huge step in getting over my broken heart. It's another thing to be forced to socialize with Blake so sud-denly like this.

"Hey, Lionel." I grab his arm. "I've got to show you something."

Thankfully, he acts like this is the most natural thing in the world as I drag him out in the hallway. "Sorry," I say quickly. "But I just had to get away."

He smiles. "That's okay. I figured you were getting stressed."

"Did it show?"

"Not at all. But I know you used to go out with Blake . . . you never talk about it, but I kind of guessed that the breakup wasn't pretty."

Lionel is a year older than me, so he was out of school when Blake and I broke up. He's never asked me much about it, and I've never told him much. Still, I've always felt he understood. He has a strong sense of empathy.

"Yeah," I admit. "And I haven't really spoken to him since then. It's a little awkward."

"So that whole TV show thing? That's for real?"

"Like I said, nothing is written in stone. But Paige is really hoping for it."

"How about you?"

I shrug. "I'm not really sure how I feel. At first I was totally opposed. But it would be a chance for me to be on a real camera crew. That would be cool."

"You might even be able to get credit for it at school."

"That'd be great."

"Are you still planning to go to the desert to shoot some photos?"

"I want to." I frown. "I wish you could come."

"Me too . . . Maybe I can cut the time in Tahoe short without offending my family too badly. Do you think you could wait until after Christmas if I can get away?"

I think about it for a second. "Sure, why not."

"Hey, Lionel," interrupts Travis, the leader of the worship team, "you got a minute to come down to my office and pick up the music for next year?"

"No problem."

Travis grins at me. "Looking good, Erin. New hairstyle?"

54

I nod. "Thanks."

"I'll be back in a few," Lionel promises.

So I go around by the stairs and take a nice long drink from the drinking fountain, trying to gather my wits before I head back into the room where everyone is still hanging out. But when I turn around I run smack into Blake and nearly jump out of my sister's boots.

"Sorry," he says quickly. "I didn't mean to scare you."

"Oh." I blink and catch my breath. "Well, you did."

"Sorry."

"It's okay." I force a tolerant smile.

"Can I talk to you?"

"Talk?" I peer curiously at him.

"Yeah."

"Right now?" I glance around, wishing that Mollie would pop in. Or that Lionel would come back.

"Do you mind?"

I shrug. "Guess not."

Blake then leads me around a corner to where some chairs are situated in an informal waiting area. "Want to sit?"

Well, I really don't. But I go ahead and sit, thinking it might help to get this over with sooner. I fold my arms across my front and just wait for him to speak.

"I've been thinking about you a lot lately, Erin."

"Oh?"

"I even wanted to call you, but I figured you'd probably hang up on me."

"Do you think I'm that rude?"

"No ... not really. I guess I just think I deserve it."

I sort of nod. "Maybe ..."

"Anyway, I just want to apologize to you. I know it's kind

of late. But I just wanted to tell you how sorry I am for being such a jerk. I've felt bad about it for a long time now."

For some reason this makes me feel better. "Well, I forgive you."

"Thanks." He brightens. "And I want you to know I've been getting ready to break up with Sonya."

I frown at him now, wondering why he's telling me this.

"I already told her I didn't think we were right for each other . . . and that I wanted to start going back to church again. I've missed that . . . and a lot of things."

"Really?" I can't help but notice that my heart is beating just a little faster.

He nods somberly. "There's so much I miss and regret."

I don't say anything. Really, I'm not positive I know what he's trying to say . . . where he's going with all this. But if it's where I think it might be, I don't want to go there.

"So when I told Sonya that, she said she wanted to come to church too."

"Really?" Okay, I realize I'm repeating myself, but this is an awkward situation.

"So I didn't want to just dump her without ever taking her to church. Because I got to thinking maybe that's what this was all about."

"What *what* was all about?" I'm confused.

"You and me breaking up."

"Huh?"

"Maybe it was so that I could bring Sonya to church. Maybe God wanted to use me to reach her. And then maybe . . . well, maybe she'll be okay without me."

"So you bring her to church and then you break up?"

"I know . . . it sounds lame."

"Ya think?" I frown at him. "If you ask me, you're developing a nasty little habit, Blake. How do you think God feels about you stringing girls along then breaking their hearts?"

He looks down at his feet. "I know, Erin … and you're right. I'm just not sure how to deal with this stuff. Sometimes if feels easier to simply get it over with quickly. But maybe that's wrong. I know I handled it wrong with you."

Okay, now I am stunned. How am I supposed to react to all this? It's particularly aggravating considering how I finally felt like I'd started to let Blake go. It's like I'm being emotionally punked right now.

Then Blake actually reaches for my hand, and just feeling him touch me sends those same old tingles down my spine, and my head starts to feel light. "Erin, I want us to get back together. I don't mean today. But after I straighten things out with Sonya."

"You mean *after* you break up with her."

"Yes. But this time I'll do it right."

I pull my hand away from his and stand up. "Do you think it's right to be talking to me like this while you and Sonya are still together?"

His brow creases. "I don't know."

"Well, I do—I know how it feels to be in Sonya's shoes." I step away from him. "I've got to go."

"Erin," he calls after me, but I just keep going. This time I head for the women's restroom. He can't follow me in there. I go into a stall and close the door, then close my eyes and just breathe deeply. I'm trying to process what just happened, but it feels like my head is spinning. Why is he doing this? And why is he doing this just when I finally seem to have made some progress? What is going on?

I'm not sure how long I stay in the bathroom, but by the time I come out, it looks like Mollie and Tony have taken off. Thankfully, Blake and Sonya are gone too. I look around for Lionel, but I don't see him, so I decide to call it a night too. Okay, it was a very weird night. I'm glad that it's over.

I try not to think about Blake as I drive home. I honestly don't know what kind of game he's playing, or to what degree he expects me to be involved, but I suddenly feel the need to keep that boy at a safe distance. For my own heart's sake as much as anything else. Sure, I was kind of pulled in there for a moment ... and I felt those old feelings rising to the surface again. But at the same time I felt a little scared too. I don't really want to be hurt again, and I don't want to be part of hurting anyone else either. Strangely enough, I was almost starting to like Sonya tonight. Her interest in the TV show seemed genuine and she was actually being nice. And if Blake dumps her like he dumped me, well, I don't know what I'll do. But, one thing's for sure; I won't go running back to him. At least I hope I won't.

Chapter
6

If anyone had told me one week ago that I'd consider participating in a fashion-driven reality TV show, I would've just laughed. Now it's not so funny. And as we're driving to meet with Helen, I'm still wondering how this whole thing transpired. Obviously, there are a number of factors at play here.

Because Paige's screen test was a success, Helen offered us a contract. For some reason the contract includes me, and for some reason Paige really wants me to do this with her. That reason is probably Mom—she is adamant that I should be involved. She says it's because this is such a great opportunity for me, but I suspect it's also because she thinks my older sister needs a babysitter. Not that she would say that, but I have a feeling Mom thinks I might be useful for keeping Paige out of trouble.

There is another factor that's pushed me toward signing this contract, and that's Blake. In the past five days he's called me about a dozen times—not that I've answered all of those calls. As it turns out, he did break up with Sonya.

"I don't know why I hurt you like that last year," he told me yesterday when I finally agreed to meet him for coffee. "I just wasn't thinking straight back then and Sonya was really persuasive."

"And you were easily persuaded," I reminded him.

"But being with her wasn't anything like being with you. You and I had fun together, Erin. We liked doing the same things. Remember our bike rides? Or going to the museum? And the video we made in the park last spring? Sonya never wanted to do anything like that. Her favorite pastime is shopping. She isn't anything like you. And it just wasn't the same."

Naturally, I didn't know how to how to respond to that. Besides wanting to say "duh" or "get a clue." Of course, it wouldn't be the same. Good grief, Sonya is a different person—how could it be the *same*? Still, I was trying to be polite.

"I've really missed you, Erin." He was looking directly into my eyes then. And it wasn't that I didn't believe him, but I think I was overwhelmed. I kept asking myself: Why this? Why now? Why can't I just move on? And what if I'm pulled back in and I get hurt all over again?

"I missed you too," I finally admitted. "But I was getting *over it*."

"I'm not over it." He reached for my hand again, and this time I didn't pull away. Part of me wanted to get up and run … but another part wouldn't move. I guess that's how it is with your first real love—it's hard to let go. "And I'm not over you," he said with sincere, dark eyes.

"This is so confusing, Blake. I really don't understand what's—"

"Maybe I needed to be with Sonya," he said. "It was like

being with her showed me how much better things were with you."

That made me want to ask him why he stuck with Sonya for so long, if that was true. Instead I just studied him, trying to discern if he was really sincere. Not that Blake is an insincere person. At least he never had been before. But this whole thing just felt a tad bit flaky to me.

"I don't know ..." I felt my more sensible side stepping in. "I think maybe what we had is gone now, Blake. I think maybe it died and just really needs to rest in peace."

He looked truly hurt then. "But I still love you, Erin. I don't think I ever stopped loving you."

Okay, he almost had me there. Despite my sensible side and my resolution not to be swept in, I could feel the tide starting to turn. This unexpected attention was flattering. Plus, it made me feel better about all those past months of being bummed and feeling rejected. Like maybe things were about to start leveling out, and life as I used to know it was about to start up again. Like that feeling of hopefulness might somehow be related to all this ... or not.

That's when I had to ask myself—if that was how Blake acted when he was supposedly still in love with me (specifically, I mean breaking my heart and dating another girl for more than half a year), why would I want to invite more of the same? Seriously, something is wrong when a guy says he never stopped loving you, but simultaneously continued dating someone else. It just doesn't ring quite true.

Still, that other part of me was caving. I wanted to believe him, I wanted to give him another try. I knew it wasn't reasonable, and I like to think of myself as a pretty grounded person. My heart does not rule my head—or at least I try not to let it.

So I pulled my hand away from his and told him that I needed to think about all of this.

Then I stood, told him good-bye, and left.

I was barely home when Blake called me again, apologizing for coming on too strong. "I wasn't trying to pressure you, Erin," he said gently. "I just wanted you to know where I'm at right now. You know?"

"I appreciate that," I told him. I was about to point out that he'd barely broken up with Sonya ... and that maybe we both needed to give this thing some time. But the next thing I knew he was asking me if I would go out with him on Friday. Was he even listening to me?

"What?" I asked, wondering if maybe I'd misunderstood or just heard him wrong.

"I thought we could spend some time together—catch up on lost time." He paused. "To start over."

I can barely describe what happened next, but it was like an alarm went off inside of me, or a red flag was frantically waving and warning me to be cautious. Maybe it was God. "I don't think I'm quite ready to start over," I told Blake.

"What's that supposed to mean?"

"It means this feels too fast ... too soon for me. I was just starting to get over you and suddenly you blast back into my life and want us to get back together. It's pretty overwhelming."

"We can take it slower," he said. "I don't want to pressure you."

"That's good," I told him. And I think that's when it hit me: if I signed the contract to do the show with Paige, I would become very busy and possibly be traveling a lot. This whole thing with Blake really helped to solidify that thought, and I made up my mind.

"Here's the deal," I said. "It looks like this TV show is really going to happen. I mean, we haven't signed the contract yet, but if my mom's lawyer gives us the green light, things will probably start moving fast. It sounds like the show will take a lot of time and we'll be traveling all over, and I just don't see how I'll have much time to be in a serious relationship." I was so surprised at how freeing it felt to say that. Like a weight was being lifted.

But I could tell Blake was disappointed, and so I suggested that we could get reacquainted through email and occasional phone calls. Although he agreed to this, I could hear the hesitation in his voice. I actually wondered if he regretted breaking up with Sonya now—and that made me mad. It also made me wonder if Blake isn't just a really needy guy—I mean, if he can't even take a breather between relationships, if he just goes hopping from one girl to the next ... well, I probably should be concerned about being in a relationship with him. Who needs another broken heart?

I've decided that if Blake really does love me (and that's a pretty big *if*) then he should be willing to take it slow and support me in doing this show with Paige. And if what he said was true—that he *never* stopped loving me—then another year or so shouldn't change anything either. Or so I'm hoping.

And that's why I made my big announcement last night. I told Paige and Mom that I was in—that I would do the show. They were so happy that we went out for ice cream to celebrate. Mom told us that her attorney, other than a few little tweaks, felt the contract was solid and good. The starting salary wasn't huge, but depending on the show's success it could get better. Plus, all the travel and expenses would be covered. But the best part, according to Paige, would be the free designer clothes. I'm guessing Paige would've agreed to this deal even if clothes were the *only* form of payment.

This afternoon we're on our way to sign the contract, but suddenly I'm feeling doubtful and insecure. What was I thinking? *A show about fashion?* That's just not me. Plus, it's hitting me anew that taking on this show means putting the brakes on my education—I'd been so excited to get into the film program at UCLA. But, like Mom says, this experience might be more valuable than taking classes, as it's doing versus seeing. She says that she's sure my academic advisors would encourage me to go for it, and that I can finish school afterward and end up with a really impressive bio. Even so, I feel nervous as we sit down for the second time in Helen Hudson's office.

"I have good news," she tells us. "The pitch was well received on the first level, and I'll be doing a follow-up pitch with the bigwigs after Christmas. Things are really moving along. I expect we'll have a decision in early January, which is a good thing considering that the Golden Globes are right around the corner."

"We'll be at the Golden Globes?" Paige's eyes are so huge that I'm sure she's imagining herself giving her first acceptance speech for an award, which is totally ridiculous considering she's never even been in anything.

"The plan is to have you on the red carpet."

"The red carpet . . ." Paige lets out a happy sigh. "This is so exciting."

"And I'm also trying to get you on an episode of *Malibu Beach*."

"*Malibu Beach*?"

"You'd be interviewing Mia Renwick and some of her friends. But I'm sure they'd like to get you involved in the storyline too. You know how they like to stir things up on that show."

"That would be awesome," Paige replies.

"You girls will have to hit the road running," Helen tells us. "Filming could begin as early as January tenth. Would you be ready?"

"Absolutely," Paige assures her.

I nod and swallow hard. Everything is happening so fast. I feel like I'm about to climb onto a wild theme park ride and that I'd better hold on tight.

Before I know it, we are signing the contracts, and as Mom and Paige discuss details, I pray that this is not all a big mistake. I suppose that sounds like I'm praying in reverse, but mostly I want to cover my bases.

We're just getting ready to leave when Sci-fi Girl (aka Sabrina the assistant) comes in. "Fran Bishop just got here," she tells Helen.

"Send her in." Then we're introduced to a girl in jeans and a T-shirt who doesn't look much older than Paige and me. "Fran will direct *On the Runway*," Helen tells us. "She's worked on several shows for me, including *Malibu Beach* most recently, and she's not only an expert on reality TV, she's really tuned into the teen market."

"I'm hoping we can get a jump start on this." Fran talks quickly, as if she's in a hurry. "We're shooting a *Malibu Beach* episode in early January. In this particular episode, we're featuring a fundraising fashion show that Mia Renwick is helping to organize — unless the whole project goes south, which is a distinct possibility that could prove just as interesting. Anyway, I'd like Paige to cover the fashion event for *On the Runway*. Sort of a cross-promotion opportunity and a chance for you girls to get a feel for this." Fran peers curiously at Paige, almost as if she's unsure of something. "Helen seems convinced that you've got the right stuff to carry this show, Paige."

"I plan to give it my best effort." Paige smiles brightly.

"I have to admit that I wasn't overly thrilled to take on a newbie," Fran tells us. "But I saw your screen test and I have to agree that you appear to have potential." She looks at me now. "And you're going to be our camera girl? Paige's sidekick, little sister, Girl Friday?"

"That seems to be the plan," I say with uncertainty.

She nods, then glances at her watch. "Well, nice to meet you girls. My assistant, Leah, will be in touch sometime after Christmas with more details." And just like that, she takes off.

"Okay, then ..." Helen stands. Once again, it's our cue to leave. "Thanks for coming in. You three have a good Christmas, and I'll see you in a week or so."

We're barely out of the building and Paige is on her phone. "I'm going to be on *Malibu Beach*!"

I try not to listen as she gushes to Kelsey about Helen's plan to go into production after Christmas. Mom puts her arm around me as we walk across the parking lot. "Are you doing okay?" she asks quietly.

"I guess. I mean, other than the fact my head is spinning and I'm wondering what I've just gotten myself into."

"I think this is going to be a growing experience for both of you," Mom tells me. "It means so much to Paige that you're on board."

As far as I can tell, Paige is in her own world as she blathers on about Mia Renwick and the Golden Globes and how this is just the beginning.

"Are we still going to Grandma's for Christmas?" I ask.

"Of course, why wouldn't we?"

"Oh, good." I sigh in relief. A trip to Grandma Hebo's rustic mountain cabin sounds like a welcome break to me. For starters, there's no TV. Cell phone reception is spotty at best. Best of all, working in our grandmother's less-than-modern kitchen, chopping firewood, shoveling snow, and sharing the ancient bathroom with four women and three old cats will provide a needed reality check for my "celebrity" sister. And it might give me time to think some things over too.

Chapter 7

Christmas comes and goes. As much as I love being at Grandma Hebo's, I feel antsy. Almost as antsy as Paige, who is acting like she'll either end up in lockdown or take up chain smoking before too long. I've never seen my sister do so much pacing and fidgeting. Maybe it's our grandmother's strong coffee. I swear that brew could grow hair on someone's chest.

"Really, Mom," Paige complains as we're outside working on our grandmother's firewood—our mom's idea, probably in hopes that it will tire us out. "I don't see why we can't go home a day early."

"You know your grandma expects us to stay the full five days." Mom swings the ax, solidly hitting the round of wood and splitting it in two, which I must admit is impressive. "It'll hurt her feelings if we leave any sooner."

"But we're leaving *tomorrow*, right?"

Mom waits as Paige picks up the split pieces. "I remember a time when you girls couldn't wait to get up here, and then you never wanted to leave."

"When we were in grade school." Paige lobs the wood toward the pile that I'm neatly stacking, nearly hitting me in the foot.

"Hey, watch it," I warn as I jump to avoid getting any broken bones.

"Sorry," she grumps back at me.

"Come on, girls," Mom urges us. "Just because you're going to be TV stars doesn't mean you have to turn into spoiled divas. Don't forget your roots."

"Yeah, right." Paige holds up her hands and frowns. "Dirt, pitch, broken nails ... like I'm a *real* diva, Mom."

"I still like being up here and helping Grandma," I say. "It's just that I wanted to make it to the desert to take photos before the show goes into production. This is supposed to be our vacation time, remember?"

"And I just want to get back to civilization to check my phone and Facebook and maybe even watch a little TV," Paige says. "I feel so disconnected up here—seriously, I think it's making me crazy."

So much for a reality check. Somehow we make it through another day, and I'm actually a little sad to leave as Grandma Hebo kisses me on the cheek. I promise to come back on my own next summer, maybe stay a few weeks if I can and get her stocked up with firewood.

"Travel safely," she tells us.

Then as we're heading home and I'm half asleep, Paige lets out a shriek that makes me think there might be a semi-truck coming straight at us.

"What?" Mom slows the car, as if she too thinks we're headed for death and disaster.

"I finally managed to get a connection!" Paige shouts.

"And there's a message from Fran Bishop."

"So?" I lean into the backseat, wishing my sister wasn't such a drama queen. Although considering what we're getting into, I suppose it's a good thing.

"What does it say?" Mom asks. "Is something wrong?"

To my surprise, I feel slightly worried. What if the show has fallen apart already? I can't believe that this actually troubles me, but it does.

"No. Something is totally right. Erin and I are invited to a New Year's Eve party that's actually going to be an episode on *Malibu Beach*!" she exclaims.

"What are we supposed to do there?" Now I'm feeling a bit unnerved. *Malibu Beach* is way out of my comfort zone.

"*Debut.*" Paige says this word in a dreamy way.

"Huh?"

"Fran says it will be our first debut on national TV, and she wants to meet with us tomorrow to give us some wardrobe and makeup direction as well as some scripting ideas." Paige makes a face. "Does Fran think we're totally ignorant or something? I know how to do wardrobe and makeup, and I certainly don't need someone telling me how to talk. I mean, it is a reality show, is it not?"

"She's probably just being careful," Mom says as she turns from the back road onto the main highway. "You girls are still new to all this. I'm sure she just wants cover all the bases."

"Or else she's worried about me," I say quietly. "Do you think Fran really expects me to go to this New Year's party too? I'm only the camera girl, right? And *Malibu Beach* isn't *our* show."

"She said *both* of us," Paige clarifies. "We're supposed to come to the studio at five o'clock tomorrow. I better call her and confirm that we'll be there."

I want to point out that this is not exactly what I'd signed on to do. I mean, agreeing to play camera girl with my sister is one thing. Making an appearance on one of the most popular (and IMO, shallowest) reality shows on TV wasn't mentioned anywhere in the contract. Although I do recall a clause agreeing to do publicity, and I suspect *Malibu Beach* might fall into that category. Still ... I am feeling more than a little nervous at the moment, and I'm wishing that I'd talked Mom into staying another day or two at Grandma Hebo's. Then I could have avoided this Malibu Barbie party altogether. Of course, Paige would've been furious.

"Those shoes do not go with that dress, Erin." Fran is pointing at my feet with a troubled expression. We're at the studio, and Fran is getting us all set for our "big night out."

"Maybe it's the dress," I suggest, since I like the shoes a whole lot better than the magenta cocktail dress that Fran has selected for me. In addition to these straps, which feel like they're slicing into my shoulders, it's so tight that I doubt I'll even be able to sit down.

"That dress happens to be a Miu Miu."

I imagine a cat with a hairball as I give her a very blank look. "Sorry, I'm not too well versed on designers."

Fran frowns at me. "Then you better start doing your homework, Erin."

"Miu Miu is Prada," Paige explains in an authoritative tone, which I'm sure is meant to impress Fran. "The Miu Miu line was originally targeted at the younger market because it was more affordable, but it's been so popular that even older women like it."

Fran nods. "That's right."

"Well, I wish this Miu Miu was a muumuu," I mutter as I struggle to shimmy the short, tight dress down my thighs to what feels a more respectable length, if that's possible.

Fran looks at me with a creased forehead. "Maybe it's not that the dress is too small, but rather you are too large."

Did she just say that? I want to throw something. I can feel Paige looking at me now, as if to say, *keep your cool, Erin ... don't fly off the handle*. But it's too late. I'm already mad. "Are you saying I have to be a size four to be on TV?"

"You said it, not me." Fran is thumbing through the dress rack now, her back toward me.

"Because I am not into the anorexia thing. Not at all. I'm just fine with my body the way it is. And if you expect me to lose weight just to be on this stupid—"

"No one's telling you to lose weight, Erin," Fran says. "Just chill, okay?"

"Well, just so you know," I continue, "I never wanted to be in *front* of the camera. I only wanted to work on the camera crew, and maybe that was a mistake."

"That's not what Helen said."

"Then maybe I should speak to Helen." I'm struggling to unzip the tight dress, deciding that it's time to make a fast getaway.

"You signed a contract, Erin." Fran looks slightly angry. "A contract some girls would kill to sign."

"I did it for Paige." I peel off the detestable dress, then just stand there feeling humiliated in my underwear, which is not nearly as cool as the underwear Paige is wearing. But why should that surprise me? "And now I regret it," I continue hotly.

"Come on, Erin." Paige urges me with a worried look. "Lighten up, will you?"

"And I'd just as soon not go to this New Year's party," I tell Fran as I hand her the dress. "I agreed to do *On the Runway* — to play my role as camera girl. I never said I'd make a fool of myself on *Malibu Beach*." Seriously, what am I doing here?

Fran takes the dress and turns away. Paige is giving me one of her big-sisterly *I'm warning you* looks. The "don't spoil this for me, or I will make you miserable." Not that I'm worried. I grab up my clothes and am starting to get dressed when Fran comes back.

"Oh, don't start getting all snippy on me, Erin." Fran actually smiles — but it's a catty smile. She's holding up a black dress with a little more coverage on top and some flare in the skirt. "This is Miu Miu too, but it's a size six. *And* I think it will go with your shoes."

"It'll look great on you," Paige says happily. "Come on, try it."

"It's a classic," Fran tells me as she takes it from the hanger and begins putting it over my head. "And maybe you are too, Erin."

Okay, I'm not sure how to react as she zips the dress, which is much more comfortable than the first one, but I'm thinking maybe Fran is a little passive-aggressive. Like that old aunt who pokes at your weight until you cry and then buys you an ice cream sundae to make you feel better. At least the black dress fits and seems to look okay — or so they are telling me.

After Paige tries on several dresses, all which look fantastic, Fran finally settles on a red number for her. It's got a name I can't begin to pronounce, but I have to admit Paige looks fabulous in it. Well, except for all the cleavage that's showing.

"So the girls are going to get a little airtime of their own, huh?" I ask my sister, pointing to her chest while Fran is consulting with the hair and makeup stylists.

Paige just laughs. "It's just a little skin. You really need to lighten up."

Well, maybe I would lighten up if I didn't know that Mom expected me to babysit. I wonder what she would say—not that she's commented too much on our clothes these past couple of years. That was Dad's domain. He always said that his daughters had too much self-respect to go out in public looking like prostitutes. Not that Paige looks like a prostitute, but she certainly doesn't look like Laura Ingalls Wilder either.

"You need to dress like ladies so you'll be treated like ladies," my dad used to tell us. I suppose his influence on me was even stronger than he knew, because I still think of his words when I pick out my clothes. I wonder if there's some way I can continue to remind Paige of Dad's wishes. Yet, when it comes to fashion, I doubt that Dad's advice carries much weight.

With shoes, dresses, and accessories finalized and bagged up for us to take home, we are back in our street clothes, moved on to hair and makeup. I sit with Vivian the makeup expert, and Paige is with Luis the hair guy.

"I try to go more natural with my makeup," I tell Vivian. Not that she's listening.

"This is a New Year's party," Fran points out from where she's standing behind me. "You're *supposed* to look glitzy and glamorous, Erin."

"That's right," Paige encourages her. "Just close your eyes and go with the flow."

"Right …" I do close my eyes. I take a deep breath and try not imagine myself being seen on national TV looking like a tramp. To my surprise, the makeup's not too terrible. A little dramatic perhaps, but for a party I suppose it's okay. And I have a feeling everyone is tired of hearing me whine. It's weird because I don't usually consider myself a complainer.

"Time to switch places," Fran announces as she continues to prep us from her notes on the latest happenings, mostly romances, on *Malibu Beach*. "Mia Renwick and Benjamin Kross are still dating," she continues, "but it got a little rocky before Christmas, and some suspect that Avery Stratton has been making moves toward Benjamin."

"Oh, I don't think so," Paige says quickly. "Avery is too nice to step in and do something like that."

"I'm just saying." Fran continues. "So here's what I'm thinking. Paige, I want you to focus on Mia since she's the one organizing the fashion show that you will be covering in your first *On the Runway* episode. Besides, it's a sure way to give you more camera time, and viewers will be curious to see how you two hit it off. Plus, Mia should be very interested in spending time with you since, no doubt, she'll want her fair share of camera time on your show."

I sleepily close my eyes as Luis puts hot curlers in my hair. I could so use a nap right now. And yet, I'm supposed to be at work, right? That's when it hits me that this is my *job*.

"Also, I thought Erin could cozy up to Avery. Maybe even find out what her interest in Benjamin is. Just for fun."

"Why would Avery even want to talk to me?" I ask without really thinking.

"Like I said, you and Paige are the new stars of *On the Runway*. Naturally, all the cast—primarily the girls—will want to score points with you. These girls are very savvy about the industry. They know *Malibu Beach* won't run forever. The smart ones are already looking for the next opportunity." Fran rambles on and I know I'm not paying as much attention as I should. Whether it's the heated rollers or the time of day, I am so sleepy that I can't imagine staying up until midnight. I wonder if I'll be able to sneak in a nap.

"Mostly I want you girls to just be yourselves," I hear Fran say as Luis begins to remove the rollers, and her voice jars me back into the present. I think I actually dozed off and I feel a little guilty. I hope I didn't snore. But Fran seems oblivious as she chatters on. "I'm starting to see why Helen wanted both of you on the show. Your personalities as well as your physical looks are actually quite complementary to each other."

I figure this is her way of saying I make Paige look even better than she already does, but I won't mention this.

"So, really, just be yourselves ... only *more* so."

"More so?" I ask Fran, hoping she thinks I've been awake this whole time. "How do you mean exactly?"

"Well, you're obviously the conservative sister. You're cautious and careful and that's okay. Go ahead and play that up. It's actually kind of cute and funny." Fran goes over to stand behind Paige, placing a hand on her shoulder. "On the other hand, Paige is more dramatic and adventuresome. She's confident and competitive and I want her to just take it up a notch."

"A notch?" Paige looks like she's noodling on this.

"Yeah, take it to the next level."

Paige's eyes narrow slightly as her brows arch—I know my sister, and this is her watch-out-for-me look. "Okay," Paige begins. "Let's say I'm talking about Mia's dress tonight. Are you suggesting I should go ahead and give my honest fashion critique and maybe a bit more?"

"Precisely." Fran nods.

"And if a catfight breaks out?" I query.

Fran just laughs. "Then a catfight breaks out. That's the nature of this beast. But the difference here is that Paige takes the high road. She plays the lady—she is simply expressing herself. She doesn't pull hair or scratch. Right, Paige?"

"I certainly hope not." Paige looks slightly worried now.

"And if she, say, manages to offend Mia?" I watch Fran consider my question.

"Then Paige simply makes light of it and moves on. It will be Mia who will end up looking silly for overreacting."

I shake my head doubtfully. Something about this plan feels half-baked. But then I wonder if that's how Fran wants it.

"Absolutely." Paige continues talking to Fran. "If a person wants to be offended, that's their choice. I will make it clear that I'm only doing my job. Just like any fashion critique, I just want to teach and make this world a more beautiful place. And, really, what's wrong with that?" She giggles as if this is some game.

"And a fashion critique doesn't get down and roll in the dirt," Fran points out.

"Yeah ... right." I try not to imagine one of those Malibu Barbies, or perhaps several of them in combined force, grabbing my fashion-expert sister by the hair and dragging her into a big, ugly fight. And if that does happen, what am I supposed to do about it? Jump in and save her?

Chapter 8

"*I think I might've fallen asleep while I was* getting my hair done," I confess to Paige as she drives us home.

"Hopefully you didn't drool." She glances at me as if to check. "Your makeup still seems to be intact."

I shake my head. "I'm just not cut out for this kind of thing, Paige. I'm worried I'm going to ruin it for you."

"You'll be fine, Erin. You just need to relax."

"According to Fran, I'm supposed to be myself," I remind her. "And I have a feeling she thinks that's an uptight, slightly neurotic worrywart."

Paige laughs. "Might make for good TV."

"Right …"

Fortunately, once we get home, we have enough time for a real nap. Even Paige thinks this is a good idea. "Just don't mess up your hair and makeup," she warns me. "Although I'm sure there will be stylists at the set—just not *our* stylists."

"Meaning they might try to make us look bad?"

"You never know." She waves her finger. "Reality television is kind of a cat-eat-cat world."

"Clever." I roll my eyes and head for my room.

But after what seems only a few minutes of sleep, someone is knocking on my door. "Hey, Erin," says Mollie as she lets herself in. "Your mom said you might be asleep."

"Yeah." I nod and sit up. "I was."

"Sorry." She holds up her hands. "But I was lonely, okay?"

"It's okay. But why are you lonely? No big plans for New Year's Eve?"

"I thought Tony and I were going out tonight. But now that's all changed." She frowns. "And it's partly your fault."

"My fault?" I sit up straighter, putting pillows behind me.

"Yeah. We were going to double with you and Blake."

"Me and Blake." I frown at her. "What are you talking about?"

"Blake thought you were going to go out with him." She sits down on my bed, releasing what seems a dismal sigh.

"But I told him—"

"I know, I know. But Blake is slightly delusional. Anyway, once he figured things out he pulled the plug on whatever it was he had planned for the four of us tonight."

"Why don't you and Tony do something anyway?" I suggest.

"Because now we don't have reservations anywhere."

"But still, you could—"

She waved her hand. "It's okay. I'm over it."

I shake my head and wonder if she came over here to make me feel guilty. And if so, why?

"But I must say, you *do* look glamorous."

I look down at my T-shirt and jeans. "Huh?"

She points to my head. "Hairdo ... makeup. Must be for the *Malibu Beach* party, huh?"

"How did you hear about *Malibu Beach*?"

"Paige's Page."

"Huh?"

"Facebook."

"Oh . . ."

"She wrote about the party. In fact, that's how Blake figured out that tonight was not going to work. I thought you already knew."

"Not really. You know, we only heard about this party yesterday," I tell Mollie.

"That's what it said on Facebook."

"So do you, like, check it out every day?" I ask.

"Not every day. But sometimes I get a tweet and then I go and check."

Okay, I don't even want to talk about Twitter. I'm so not into that. I mean, seriously, why is everyone out there blabbing about everything? Sometimes I wonder what would happen if all our cell phones, IMs, emails, and all that just vanished. Would everyone go nuts, or would we learn how to just have a normal conversation? Of course, I can't say this to Mollie because she's so into all that. Maybe I was just born into the wrong generation. Or I'm "conservative," as Fran told me earlier today.

"And Paige is really getting a lot of fans too."

"Fans?" I try to wrap my head around how Paige can possibly have *fans* when she doesn't even have a show yet.

"Fans, friends, whatever. I think she has about five thousand on Facebook now."

"You're kidding!"

"The Wonderland spot was one of the most-watched YouTube videos."

"It's on YouTube?"

"Do you like live under a rock, Erin?"

I scowl at her. "I have other interests."

Mollie frowns. "Don't you ever check these sites out?"

I just shrug. "Not really."

"And you should probably get your own page too, Erin."

I get out of bed now. I look at myself in the mirror, trying to estimate how much damage I may have done to my makeup and hair. It actually looks pretty much the same as it did earlier, and I'm sure Paige can fix whatever doesn't.

"Is that what you're wearing tonight?" Mollie is looking at the garment bag hanging on my closet door.

"Yeah, it's called meow meow or something like that."

"What?" Mollie gives me a weird look. "Can I see it?"

"Sure. Go ahead."

While she's unzipping the bag I make a trip to the bathroom. It's already after seven and the limo is supposed to get us at seven thirty. Okay, this is so surreal that I can't even wrap my head around it. How weird is it that I'm going to a *Malibu Beach* party, dressed to the nines, and riding in a limo?

"Are you getting ready?" Paige calls from the kitchen where she's getting herself a soda.

"I guess."

"I already touched up my makeup and hair," she says. "I'll come in and look at yours in a few minutes."

When I return to my room, Mollie is standing in front of my mirror, holding the black dress up like she's wearing it.

"Kind of boring, isn't it?" I say as I close the door.

"Boring?" She turns and gives me an are-you-crazy look.

"I mean, the dress isn't that interesting. But it's what fit me."

"It's pretty. And it's not a meow meow. It's a Miu Miu."

"Isn't that what I said?" I say with a smile. I start removing my clothes, trying not to mess my hair, thinking about what the hair guy said about wearing a button-up shirt next time.

"I'm trying really hard not to be jealous." Mollie hands me the dress with a sad little smile.

"Hey, if there was a way I could trade places, I would."

She nods. "Yeah . . . you probably would." Now she brightens. "And maybe if Paige's show is a big hit, you'll be able to invite some of your friends to join you sometimes. You think?"

"I don't see why not." Even as I say this, I have no idea. Still, I hate to see Mollie feeling bad. "Hey, how did the commercial go?"

"I don't know. They used several girls for it. I might end up on the cutting-room floor."

"You and me both," I tell her as she zips up my dress.

"I doubt that."

Then Mollie sits down and watches as Paige comes in, all dressed and looking like absolute perfection. Naturally, Mollie makes a big deal about this. Paige then repairs the damage I apparently did to my hair, and finally hands me a small purse. "I equipped it with lip gloss and powder just in case the *Malibu Beach* stylists are too busy to help us."

And before long, Mom is calling us to say that the limo has arrived. Then, as if we're going to the prom, she insists on taking our pictures before we leave. I'm actually a little surprised that she didn't want to come with us, but since she's dressed up too, I'm guessing she has other plans.

"Have fun on your big date," Paige says to Mom as we're heading out with Mollie trailing us like a lost puppy.

"Big date?" I echo, but Paige ignores me.

Mom calls out thanks as we traipse down the stairs, and

reminds us that she's got her cell phone in case we need to call. "It'll be on," she says, as if she might be worried about us being on our own for New Year's. Or maybe she thinks we're worried about her.

"Mom's going on a date?" I ask my sister after I've said good-bye to Mollie. Paige and I are sitting in back of the limo now, which is really just a town car, but kind of fun just the same. "A real date with a real guy?"

Paige simply nods as she rechecks herself in the mirror of her compact. Like she's not perfect?

I simply cannot believe my mom is going out with someone. This is a first and I'm not sure how I feel about it. Not that anyone seems to care about my opinion lately.

"Who with?" I try to sound casual as I ask.

"A guy at work. She said it's not really a date—but I'm not so sure."

"Have you met this guy?"

"No. But I think his name is Tom. Or Tim. Or maybe it's Jim."

"Right …" I try not to worry about my mom being on a date, or the fact that our big debut could easily blow up in our faces if my sister offends one of the Malibu Barbies. *Don't worry … just pray*, I remind myself.

And before I know it, the car is passing through the security gate, and there are tents and camera crews around. I feel like my stomach is tying itself into knots. *Malibu Beach* is supposed to be the edgiest reality show for teens yet. Besides the casual use of alcohol (don't let those plastic red cups fool you), there are rumors that some of the cast are experimenting with drugs and who knows what else. I'm *so* not ready for this. Then the town car stops and, although it seems too soon to be in Malibu, the door opens, but instead of us getting out, it's Fran getting in.

"You girls ready to rock and roll?" she asks as she opens a bag and starts removing what I can tell is sound equipment. "We wanted to get you wired up with mics before you arrive at the scene. It makes it easier for the guys to just start shooting, getting your natural reactions and all that."

As we fumble with the wires and small microphones, trying to conceal them beneath our dresses — which is no small feat — Fran continues to brief us about the evening.

"Now remember, although our own camera crew is there on the grounds, they won't be allowed into the actual party because that's where the *Malibu Beach* crew is already set up to film, and there's only so much room. The truth is they can get kind of territorial. So you girls have to make the most of it before we go onto the actual party. My guess is that some of the *Malibu Beach* cast will want some camera time with you girls and our crew too, hoping that they can get seen on your show. Remember these girls are opportunistic. Just make the most of it, okay?"

"No problem," Paige says with confidence.

"Right." I bite my lip and prepare myself for the worst.

"And don't be nervous," Fran tells me as we pass through some security gates, and the driver slows then finally parks. "I'll be around if you need anything. Act like yourselves, like you're guests at a party."

Then someone is opening the car door, and I watch as Paige slowly extends a long leg out, just in time for a camera to catch her emerging from the car like a star. In comparison, I feel like a klutz, and as I catch my heel and nearly fall on my face, I hear trickles of laughter from what I can only assume are cast members . . . people in formal clothes, clustered here and there as if trying not to appear too obvious as they watch us.

"Hey there, little sister." Paige reaches for my hand to steady me, using a voice that I can tell is for the cameras. "I guess we should've cut you off sooner. But then it is New Year's Eve . . . time to party." This is followed by more laughter. At my expense, I'm sure. Hopefully none of this camera footage will make it into the actual show. I glare at my "big" sister and try to remember that she's probably hamming it up for the sake of our TV show. But what if she pushes it too far? How much will be too much? And am I supposed to challenge her?

"The Forrester sisters," says a very pretty blonde that I'm guessing is Mia Renwick, but since I don't watch the show, I could be wrong. Ironically, she too has on a red dress. Two diva-type blondes wearing two similar dresses. Not good. And, although I'm not a fashion expert, I can tell that Mia doesn't look nearly as hot as Paige. I suspect Paige is thinking the same thing.

Paige just smiles and goes directly to the girl. "Hey, Mia," she says like they're old friends.

"Paige," Mia says as she takes her hand and they exchange air kisses. I try not to laugh at how ridiculous that looks.

"And this is my little sister, Erin."

Mia barely looks at me, but nods as if to say, "it's okay, she can come too." Then she leads Paige over to meet some of her friends. Naturally, the cameras stick with this group—the A list. I should be relieved for this little break, but instead, feeling like a party crasher or maybe just a misfit, I follow behind and watch from a safe distance. The girls seem to assess Paige with a sort of bored interest, but I suspect it's only an act.

I suspect they're thinking, like I am, that she is outshining Mia Renwick. Then again, they might simply be planning how to get their own moment with Paige. Like Fran said, *Malibu Beach* won't last forever.

"Hi," a petite brunette says to me quietly. "You must be the sister."

"I feel like the ugly stepsister," I admit, then glance over my shoulder to be sure we're not on camera.

She laughs. "I feel like that sometimes too. You probably know that I'm Avery Stratton. I'm pretty much used to living in Mia's shadow on this show."

"I'm Erin Forrester," I tell her.

"The funny thing is that Mia and I actually *really* were friends before the show began. Best friends, if you can believe it."

"So did the show mess that up?"

Avery nods sadly. "That and so much more."

"Oh."

"And being that you're a sensible girl—that's what I've heard anyway—you probably wonder why I stuck with the show, right?"

"Sort of."

"I'll give you one guess."

"Money?"

Avery laughs. "Well, you may not be a star, but you are a smart girl."

"You know what they say, follow the money. My next guess would've been boys."

"Another good guess. And, like everyone else, you've probably heard that Mia thinks Benjamin and I are sneaking around."

"Are you?"

Avery gives me a sly look, then glances around to make sure we're not being filmed, which doesn't appear to be the case since both crews are still glued to Paige and Mia, the stars. "We try to give the viewers what they want." She casually waves to a guy who's just coming out of one of the tents. "You will too."

"Who's that?" I ask as nonchalantly as possible.

"Are you kidding?"

"Let me guess—Benjamin Kross?"

"You don't watch our show much, do you?" She looks truly shocked and maybe even slightly offended.

But I just shrug. "Not so much. Sorry."

Benjamin is coming over to us. He and Avery exchange a friendly kiss, which surprises me since Mia, his supposed girlfriend, is only about ten feet away. But then, maybe that's just the norm around here. As Avery introduces us, I notice Benjamin has a red plastic cup in his hand, like most people at the party. It's amazing to me that they'd be so casual about drinking with cameras running.

"And that's Erin's sister over there," Avery tells Benjamin.

He nods as if he approves. "How do I get an introduction to her?" He seems to direct this query to me, and so I take the initiative and walk him over to meet Paige. Knowing that cameras are rolling, I manage to introduce them without botching it too badly.

"Benjamin," Paige says with a twinkle in her eye. "It's nice to meet you."

"You too." He grins, then holds out his arms like he's about to say *tah-dah!* "So, tell me, how did I do? Would I make your fashion do's or don'ts list?"

Paige looks him up and down, then smiles with approval. "Oh, you are definitely a *do*."

He chuckles. "I'll hold you to that."

"And how about the rest of us?" A tall girl in a bright blue dress steps up. She has long, nearly black hair and is wearing gigantic silver hoops in her ears. "Which list would the rest of us make?"

"Would you like me to start with you?" Paige asks, not missing a beat.

"Yes," says another girl. "Do Natasha."

"Why not?" Natasha strikes a poise, confidence exuding from her. And really, she looks like she could be a professional model. Tall, thin, stately.

Paige smiles sweetly as she carefully looks her over. "The color of your dress is superb on you," she begins. "It really makes your eyes sparkle and brings out the best in your complexion. Great choice."

"Thank you." Natasha smiles

"But the cut is unflattering."

"Unflattering?" Natasha's smile evaporates.

"See how it sags a bit here." Paige points to the loose fabric along the sides of her midriff. "Not very attractive. A slight alteration would've helped ... maybe. Although this fabric, in this cut ... well, it's only my opinion, but it was probably a mistake from the get-go."

Mia laughs. "I have to agree with her, Natasha. That dress makes you look totally flat on top and kind of hippy on the bottom. I was going to tell you myself, but I never got the chance."

"Sorry," Paige says brightly. "You asked."

"What about Mia's dress," Natasha demands. "Tell us what you think of *that*."

Paige looks at Mia innocently. "Oh, I don't know ..."

"Come on," Benjamin urges her. "I'd like to hear this too." He steps next to Paige, cupping his chin in his hand, appearing to study his girlfriend's red dress, which is similar to Paige's but not quite right. At least I don't think it is, but then again, I'm no expert.

Mia just shrugs. "Go for it, Paige. I'd be interested to hear what you think."

Paige presses her lips together, then nods. "Well, for starters, some blondes look good in a true red ... and some just don't. It has to do with your skin tone and eye color. And, don't feel badly, Mia, but you're one of the blondes that should just say no to red. It washes you out." Paige smiles. "You don't hate me now, do you?"

"Of course I don't hate you." Mia frowns slightly. "And I suppose *you* can wear red?"

Paige ignores Mia as she turns to Benjamin. "What do you think? You know Mia better than anyone here, right?"

Benjamin looks at Mia and then at Paige, then back to Mia. "I think you nailed it, Paige. Mia does look kind of pale, like she's not feeling so great." He puts his hand on her forehead. "Still nursing that hangover from the weekend, are we?"

Several people laugh, but Mia pushes his hand away. "Paige didn't answer my question," she says to him. "Why don't you answer it for her. Do you think Paige is a blonde who *can* wear red?"

He gives a sheepish smile. "Oh, yeah, I think Paige can wear red just fine."

I can tell Mia is *seeing* red now. And it looks like she's not going to give up on this. "So what about the cut of this dress, Paige? Anything you'd like to say about *that*?" Mia stands straighter now, holding her head high and exposing even more cleavage than my sister, which in a weird way is kind of a relief. Maybe Dad wouldn't be upset after all.

"It's an *okay* cut," Paige begins slowly, as if she's watching her step. "But I have to say that dress is not particularly well made." She points to some tucks and seams along the front of the dress. "This workmanship is a little shoddy."

"*Shoddy?*" Mia looks at Paige like she's lost her mind. "Do you have any idea *who* made this dress, or what it costs?"

"I can take a guess." Paige studies the dress even more closely. "I think it's a Badgley Mischka—"

"That's right," snaps Mia. "And I can't believe you'd call it shoddy. Do you realize that the cameras are on? And that you have just insulted one of the finest designers around?"

"You didn't let me finish," Paige says sweetly. "I was about to say that it looks like a Badgley Mischka *knockoff.*"

"That's ridiculous." But Mia looks uncomfortable, and I'm thinking my sister is right.

"Maybe you haven't heard there are some counterfeits floating around this area," Paige tells her. "My guess is that's one of them. If you'd like, we could examine the label and determine—"

"Thank you, but no thank you." Mia seems to force a stiff smile. "Now, how about if I critique *your* dress?"

Paige nods. "Go for it."

Mia looks at Paige, but she just stands there and it seems she has nothing to say. How could she? Paige looks perfect.

"Oh, come on, Mia." Benjamin goes over and nudges his girlfriend playfully, giving her a little half-smile. "Just admit it, Paige looks great. Get it over with and let's get into the party while there's still food left. I'm starving."

Mia turns and storms off toward one of the tents.

"She's probably going to change her dress," one of her friends says quietly.

"She was already mad that Paige's dress was red like hers," Natasha informs everyone.

"And I told her to wear the white one instead," another girl says.

"Did I really offend her?" Paige asks innocently. "I was only being honest and she wanted my advice. I hope I didn't hurt her feelings."

Avery steps in. "The gown *was* a knockoff," she tells Paige. "And Mia knows it."

They all laugh loudly at this, and it seems the storm has passed. But I can't help but wonder about Mia's so-called friends. Maybe Avery was right when she said this show messes up a lot of things. What a price to pay for fame and a bit of money.

Benjamin links arms with Paige. "Let me escort you to where the *real* party is about to begin." Naturally, the others sort of glom onto the unexpected couple, and, like a herd of sheep, they head through the garden and toward the house, which looks as big as a hotel.

I follow the group at a distance, noticing that the cameras are still running, cameramen jogging to keep up and grab the right shots. I wonder what Mia is going to say about this, and whether Paige is in over her head.

Chapter
9

"*Your sister knows how this thing works,* right?" Avery asks me once we're inside the foyer of the house, which still looks more like a hotel than an actual home.

"What thing?"

"The *show*."

I half shrug. "I guess she does. I mean, we were sort of briefed on it earlier today. Our director said to just be ourselves ... only more so."

Avery laughs. "That sounds about right."

"And Paige watches *Malibu Beach*. Whenever she talks about it, she sounds like an expert to me."

"Good." Avery nods. "And just so you know, the director wants the initial party conversations to start here in the foyer. We'll hang here for a while and when we get the cue, we'll start moving toward the great room over there." She nods to an open area off to our right.

"So even though this unscripted, it's sort of staged?" I question.

"Absolutely. Otherwise it would turn into chaos." She kind of laughs. "Sometimes it does anyway."

"How do they handle that?"

"The editors manage to work it all into one fairly cohesive show. It's actually kind of impressive."

"Sounds interesting."

"Anyway, we should probably move closer to the action," she directs me. "We need to at least appear interested in the key characters."

We stand nearby and watch as Benjamin and Paige continue to talk and banter and seemingly hit it off. Whether their behavior is for the cameras or for real is anyone's guess, but there is clearly some flirting going on, and it seems to be coming from both directions.

"What about Mia?" I ask Avery with uncertainty.

"Meaning where is she?"

"Sort of . . . but more like, will she be jealous?"

"Of course."

"So are the relationships—like Mia and Benjamin—for real? Or are they just hyped up for the show?"

Avery turns and looks at me like she can't believe I don't know this, but I honestly don't totally get it. "Be assured, Erin, Mia and Ben are really dating. They've been together for almost two years now and Mia is pretty sure that they'll get married."

"But isn't Mia only eighteen?"

Avery nods. "Yes. And Benjamin is only twenty."

"That seems pretty young to be thinking about marriage."

"Well, it's not like Mia's planning her wedding." Avery glances over to the entrance as if she expects Mia to charge in here at any moment.

"Didn't I hear that Benjamin has a movie contract?" I can't

believe I actually remembered a bit of *Malibu Beach* trivia. Probably from something Paige said when I was half asleep.

"Yes, and that's just one more thing Mia's not too thrilled about."

"She's not happy for Benjamin?"

"She's upset that she hasn't been offered a deal yet."

I'm tempted to make a prima donna comment about Mia, but then remember that Avery is her friend. Although I'm not so sure about how these girls define the word *friend*. I have a feeling it's more a term of convenience than endearment.

I see a couple of guys coming our way now. Obviously they're from the show so they know Avery, but I can see them looking at me. Probably wondering why someone like me has sneaked onto their show. At least they're smiling.

"So, are you going to introduce us to your new friend?" the tall dark-haired guy asks Avery. I can feel him looking at me in a way that doesn't make me feel particularly comfortable.

"You already know who she is." Avery rolls her eyes for my benefit. "Everyone on the show knew that you and Paige were coming today." Suddenly, I notice one of the cameras is focused on us now. "This is Vince Stewart." She nods to the tall guy. Then she smiles at the shorter one. "And this is Juan Romero. And this, as you know, is Erin, the younger sister."

"Pleasure to meet you." Juan shakes my hand and then slips his arm around Avery as if they are a couple.

Now Vince shakes my hand, holding a bit longer than necessary. "Nice to meet you, Erin. How about you save me a dance once someone starts breaking the ice on the dance floor?" He chuckles as he holds up a red cup. "Which reminds me, I need a refill. Can I get you something, Erin?"

"No, thanks," I tell him. "I'm fine."

"Oh, oh," Vince says. "Look who's coming."

We all turn to see Mia entering the foyer. Her red dress has been exchanged for a white one. Even I can see it's an improvement, but in my opinion she still doesn't look as good as my sister. She seems to have regained her cool, else she's just a good actress. She goes directly to Benjamin, moving into the small crowd and taking his arm with a look in her eyes that suggests ownership. Benjamin just smiles, but it seems like a placating smile, like he's only humoring her. Is it just me or is that a red flag?

"Would you like to comment on this dress?" Mia asks Paige in a loud voice that sounds more like a challenge than an invitation.

But Paige just smiles.

"What, no critique, no fashion suggestions? No hints as to whether I'll make Paige Forrester's do's or don'ts list tomorrow?"

"It looks lovely, Mia," Paige assures her. "Like a princess."

Mia doesn't seem to like this. "A *princess*? As in too sweet? Too little girlish?"

Paige looks like she's weighing her response, although I can't tell which way the scale is tipping. "Well, it's much better than the knockoff."

Mia looks like she wants to punch my sister. Instead she seems to tighten her grip on her boyfriend. "Benjamin," she says sweetly, "isn't it about time to go inside and dance?"

He nods, and they begin to head toward the great room with cameras trailing closely behind. Before they enter the room, he turns and smiles brightly. I think I see why he's getting a movie contract, because this guy knows how to light up a room. "Hey, Paige," he calls back, "don't forget that you promised me a dance."

She gives him a little finger wave and a nod, and Mia gives my sister a look so chilly that it could freeze a hot cup of coffee.

Eventually, we all meander into the great room, which is huge. When we get inside I hear music from a live band, which is situated outside on a huge deck with the beach and ocean behind them.

The next thing I know, Vince is tugging me out to the dance floor where Mia and Benjamin and several other couples, including Paige and a good-looking blond guy, are already dancing. It's not that I don't like to dance, but I'm not too impressed with Vince. I would've appreciated the chance to say, "no, thanks." But with cameras running, I don't really want to create a scene (and draw unwanted attention to myself) by ditching this guy out here on the dance floor, so I comply.

After a while I have to admit that although I didn't like my first impression, Vince is not a bad dancer. When we finish our dance, he starts questioning me about our upcoming show, asking me what my role is going to be.

"I plan to stay behind the scenes as much as possible," I tell him.

"Why would you do that?" he demands, like I'm nuts.

"Because I'm more interested in filming and producing," I explain. "Paige is the star."

He nods as he watches my sister from a distance. Right now she's dancing with Benjamin and Mia is with the blond guy—they must've traded partners. The cameras seem to be eating this up, and I can see why since the expression on Mia's face is priceless. It's like she's trying to act like it's no big deal, but she's seething.

"Oh, yeah," Vince says with approval, "that sister of yours has definitely got star quality going on." Then he smiles at me. "So can you get her to dance with me?"

Well, why should this surprise me? I shrug as if it's the most natural thing in the world for people to use me to access my sister. And maybe it is. "You'd have to ask her."

"But you could introduce me," he suggests.

"Okay," I agree. "I'll introduce you if you'll tell me what's in that cup."

He looks down at his red cup, then grins. "I thought you knew."

"I'm guessing it's not punch."

"Oh, it's punch all right. But punch with a little more punch."

"And your producers don't mind?"

"We have a don't-ask-don't-tell policy." He chuckles.

"And no one gets in trouble?"

"No more than they do on the outside."

"Meaning?"

"Meaning kids drink, you know, and sometimes they mess up with it. And sometimes"—he takes a big swig—"they don't."

"Right ..." I'm sure my skepticism is written all over my face.

"Hey, don't be all self-righteous," he warns me. "The kids in this show know how to handle themselves. They know how to stay out of trouble."

"And so the stories we hear about teenage stars doing rehab are just made up?" I counter. "Publicity stunts, perhaps?"

He chuckles. "Maybe so. Anyway, our producers know that it loosens the cast up to have a drink or two ... and that's what they want ... and so I think they just look the other way."

"As in ignorance is bliss?"

He nods. "So I answered your question. How about introducing me to Paige?"

"One more question." I nod over to where Paige is just starting the next dance with Benjamin. "Since she's occupied."

Vince looks slightly irritated. "Fine. But what are you anyway? Some kind of investigative reporter, trying to get the inside story?"

I nod. "Yeah, maybe so. But I'll protect my sources, okay?"

He grins. "Okay, shoot."

"So, tell me, Vince, why do you need to drink to loosen up? If you're an actor, like most of your cast members claim, why can't you just act like you're loosened up?"

His brow creases. "You know, that's a pretty good question."

"How about a pretty good answer then?"

"Hmmm ..." He looks over the crowd as if searching for the answer. "Maybe it's because we're not really actors."

I nod. "Maybe so."

"Now, let's make our way over there" — he nods to a corner of the room where the action seems to be happening — "and you can let your sister know that you want to talk to her. Okay?"

"Okay." I'm mulling his response in my head as we start for the other side of the room. When we're about halfway over there, I start to hear voices getting louder, but I'm too short to see exactly what's going on. Ironically, as the voices get louder the music gets quieter — and I'm wondering if the band has been directed to reduce the volume when something "interesting" develops on the set.

"Get your own freaking boyfriend!" It sounds like Mia's voice.

"You need to just chill, Mia." This sounds like Benjamin, and it's not quite as loud as Mia's, but equally intense. "This jealousy routine of yours is not attractive."

With Vince's help, I push my way through the crowd of onlookers, and am not all that surprised to see that Paige, Mia, and Benjamin are in the center of things. It's almost as if this scene has been rehearsed. If Avery hadn't told me that Mia and Benjamin were really a couple, I'd think this was just a staged scene for the sake of the viewers. Even now, I'm not totally sure. I mean, what is reality TV here and what is not?

Mia steps closer to Paige, jutting out her chin and swinging her pointer finger practically in my sister's nose. "What's the deal anyway?" Mia says with slurred words. "You can't find your own guy? So you come here and try to steal mine?"

"Mia—"

"Shut up, Benjamin!" Mia shoots at him. "You keep out of this!"

"We were only dancing," Paige attempts.

"You shut up too," Mia shrieks.

"You need to relax." Benjamin is trying to get Mia's elbow, as if he plans to escort her out.

But she does a quick flip around, freeing herself from Benjamin and lunging at Paige. "Witch!" she screams. "I'm gonna tear you to—"

"*Stop it!*" Benjamin leaps, grabbing Mia from behind and catching her by the back of her dress. The onlookers have what seems to me to be an unlikely response. Kind of like they expected a catfight and are disappointed, or maybe they're surprised at Benjamin, as if they expected him to let his girl-friend attack my sister.

Paige is backing away and she looks honestly scared. "I'm sorry, Mia," she says quietly. "I was really only dancing with—"

"Shut your face!" Mia screams as she struggles to free herself from her boyfriend. Meanwhile, he's holding on like he's got a tiger by the tail. I'm surprised no one's helping him and I'm a little worried Mia is going to get away and seriously hurt my sister.

"Help Benjamin," I command Vince. And to my surprise, he jumps in to restrain Mia. In the meantime I run over and stand by Paige and am surprised that she actually holds onto me as if I could protect her—pretty funny when you consider she's a lot taller than me.

"Back off," I tell Mia.

"Shut up, Nerd Girl!" She shakes her fist in a wobbly sort of way, like she really is drunk. At the same time she eyes me like I've just made her hit list. But I can see that she's kind of weaving back and forth and I doubt that she's going to be standing on her feet much longer.

"You're drunk," I tell her. "And maybe when you're sober, you'll remember all this and you'll see what a fool you made of yourself and learn how to—"

"You're jus' jealous," she slurs at me, "you wannabe. You wish you was beaut-a … beaut … you know whadda mean, Nerd Girl. You wish you were pretty like me."

Despite her drunkenness and the fact that she doesn't look the least bit pretty at the moment, the jab still stings. And it doesn't help when everyone laughs at this.

"Let's get her out of here," Benjamin says to Vince. Now

Juan joins them and the three guys manage to drag Mia away. Naturally, some of the cameras are trailing them, and we can hear her screaming and cussing all the way. As I turn to Paige, and notice that her face is paler than usual, I mildly wonder if her network allows that kind of language to go on the air.

"Are you okay?" I ask my sister.

"Yeah, but that was a little freaky."

"What did you do to get her so mad?" I notice that the cameras are on us now, but I don't even care.

"I was just dancing with Benjamin."

"Dancing way too close," Natasha informs Paige in a snarky tone. "What did you expect Mia to do?"

"To have a little dignity," I toss back.

"Did you even *see* your sister?" Natasha shoots back at me.

"I don't have to see Paige to know she wouldn't be—"

"She totally threw herself at Benjamin." Natasha's hands are on her hips and she steps closer to me, making me wonder if she plans to pick up where Mia left off. What is wrong with these girls anyway?

"Paige doesn't need to throw herself at anyone," I say calmly.

"She was *all over* him!" Natasha is bent down and locking eyes with me, perhaps to remind me that she too is a lot taller than I am. The truth is I am intimidated.

"Maybe you should take a look at the film footage." I nod toward the cameras. "It's all recorded, you know. Cameras don't lie."

Surprisingly this seems to quiet her. But now a girl I barely met steps in. From what I remember, her name is Brogan, and I know she's tight with Mia. I've noticed that when Brogan's not glaring at someone (like now) she's pretty, in a dark, sultry sort of way.

"Why don't you two go back to wherever it is you came from?" Brogan says. "You're not part of this group and it seems rather obvious that you're not wanted here."

"We were invited here," Paige tells her.

"Maybe it's time to *uninvite* you." Natasha seems to have revived now. She makes a sly smile and I notice the camera tightening in on her again, and I'm reminded of why we're here.

"Maybe you're acting this way for Mia's sake because she's your friend," I say to both of them, "or maybe you're just trying to get your share of the limelight tonight. But you might be embarrassed tomorrow."

Brogan laughs. "You're one to talk about embarrassment, *Nerd Girl*."

I stand a little straighter. "I might look like a nerd to you, but at least I can face myself in the morning ... or when this show airs." I turn to Paige. "I don't know about you, but I've had enough of this so-called party."

Paige still looks uneasy, but she nods. "Yeah, let's get out of here."

And, okay, it seems a bit strange, but I kind of feel like a hero as we leave. Like maybe Mom was right—maybe Paige does need me around to help keep her out of trouble.

On the other hand, maybe I'm not so different than these drama queens who think they're actually actors. Maybe I'm just fooling myself too.

Chapter
10

The cameras remain on us as we exit the party. I hold my head high—or as high as I can compared to Paige—as we walk out. Although it's a New Year's party and we didn't even make it to midnight, I am so glad this is over. But no sooner are we outside than this older guy with a goatee and wire-rimmed glasses comes over and wants to talk to us.

"You girls were great in there," he tells us.

I just frown, but Paige suddenly brightens. "Really?"

"Absolutely." He smiles and shakes our hands. "I'm Rod Spencer and I've been watching the whole thing out here on the monitors. I'm the director of *Malibu Beach*, and I gotta say you girls really spiced things up tonight."

"Well, thanks." Paige seems to be regaining her old confidence again.

He turns to me. "And what you said to Mia, Natasha, and Brogan was classic." He pats me on the back. "Pure classic."

I want to ask him what exactly he means by "classic," but he turns away and tightens his focus on Paige, encouraging her to stay for the rest of the party. "I can promise you that you'll get a lot of miles out of this." He nods with enthusiasm. "Your producer, Helen, is a good friend of mine and I promised her to give you as much camera time as possible. You stick around and you'll get it. Especially now that Mia is over in the tent puking her guts out. We have room for another star tonight."

My sister is convinced that this is a great opportunity, and she takes me aside and tells me that we owe it to our show to take full advantage of it. And the next thing I know we turn around and head back into the party. I so want to scream. But then I get an idea.

"Wait a minute," I tell her. "What about our show?"

"What do you mean? This *is* for our show."

"Not really." I pull her aside, fully aware that we're still mic'd and cameras are still rolling. "Once we step through those doors, we belong to *Malibu Beach*. But out here, we can still be filmed for *On the Runway*." I glance over to the camera guys that Fran didn't even bother to introduce us to, but who I know are here to film us.

"So what are you saying?" Paige looks confused. "That you and I hang out here and enjoy a party of two?"

"No." I look toward the house. "I'm saying we get the word out in there that we can continue conversations out here, whether it's about fashion or whatever, and maybe some of the cast would like to join us."

"I don't know." Paige shakes her head. "Why would they want to—"

"Because you're Paige Forrester," I remind her, "host of *On the Runway*."

"That's right," the bald *Runway* camera guy tosses our way. And the other one gives us a thumbs-up. I suspect it's been a pretty boring night for them.

"Only this time, maybe you could tone down the criticism," I suggest. "Let's not make any more enemies, okay?"

She looks skeptical.

"You could turn it more into interviews," I try. "Find out more about these girls, what makes them tick, and why they like being on the show. Then talk about fashion."

"I don't know ..."

"Do you want me to go find Fran and ask her?" I suggest. "I'm sure she'd back us up—"

"No ... that's not necessary." Paige nods like the light just went on. "I think you are right, Erin."

"Okay, then. How about if I try to get Avery and some of the more-reasonable girls to come out from the party to chat with you?"

"Sounds good." Paige smoothes her hair and straightens her shoulders.

Just then a couple of girls from the cast are strolling toward the house from the tent area. My guess is they've just been retouching their makeup and hair. "In the meantime, why don't you snag those two and see if they want some *On the Runway* time?"

And just like that Paige turns on her bright smile and waves. "Hey, Cassie and Giselle, you girls are looking really hot tonight."

So, hoping that maybe we'll have things somewhat under control, I hurry back inside where the music is playing again. I can't help but notice that the action on the dance floor seems a little halfhearted, and the crowd has thinned. I'm worried that some of the cast might be blaming Paige and me for that. I nervously glance around the room, shooting up a silent prayer that Natasha and Brogan won't spot me, corner me, and pull my hair out. Just then I see Avery and another girl talking. I head straight for them and quickly explain this opportunity.

"So you're inviting me to come out and be trashed by Paige?" Avery frowns like I'm nuts.

"No, Paige is going to keep it positive this time. It's going to be more like an interview. And if it goes well, maybe it'll make it on our first show." Okay, even as I say this, I have no idea, but it's worth a shot. Plus, it keeps Paige and me from getting stuck in their crazy party, which I'm afraid will only get worse if the drinking and catfights continue.

Before long, Paige has a cluster of girls and guys around her, and I can't help but be impressed with how easily she charms them with her wit and humor. She's dishing out compliments like hors d'oeuvres and everyone seems to be eating them up. Fortunately for us, but maybe not so much for Mia, we learn that Mia's still not feeling so well and that her mother's been called to pick her up.

I can only imagine how pathetic the party must be now. We can still hear the band playing, however, so maybe some people are still having a good time. Finally, Natasha and Brogan come out to see what's going on. To my relief, they keep a distance, hanging on the sidelines with sour expressions.

"Do you guys want to be interviewed?" I eventually ask them, trying to offer an olive branch of sorts. "It might be used for our show."

Natasha still seems to be pouting, but Brogan looks mildly interested. "So when is your show going to air anyway?"

"Probably not for years, if at all." Natasha narrows her eyes at me.

"I'm not sure of the exact date," I admit. "But I know we're supposed to cover the fashion show that Mia is helping with.

And we'll be at the Golden Globes ... so I'm thinking our initial air date can't be too far out."

Brogan smiles and extends her hand. "Sorry I tore into you in there, Erin," she says quietly. "You actually nailed it ... I *was* trying to catch some camera time. It's not always easy, you know."

"Don't worry about it. And anyway, that's just the kind of thing that Paige is asking people about tonight," I tell her. "She's getting to know the cast of *Malibu Beach*." Then without wasting time, I walk Brogan over, and although Paige looks a bit surprised she jumps right in and runs with it.

"I have to say, Brogan," Paige begins warmly, "I really love your dress. You want to tell us about it? My guess is that it's BCBG, am I right?"

Brogan nods. "Absolutely."

"One of my favorite designers." Paige nods. "And I have to say the color and cut are perfect."

"How did you learn so much about fashion?" Brogan asks her.

"I study it with a crazed obsession." Paige laughs. "My mom says that I'd be a scholar by now if I put half that much effort into academics. But think about it—books or dresses ... which is more fun?"

"Dresses for sure."

They both laugh as if they're old friends, and I lean back against a pillar and sigh in relief. After about an hour, everyone seems happy and friendly and we all decide to head back inside to get some food and enjoy the music. Our two camera guys, who I have learned are named Alistair and JJ, decide to wrap it up too. I suspect they have their own New Year's parties to go to.

As we're heading inside, I notice that Rod Spencer, the *Malibu Beach* director, is standing off in the shadows with another guy. And they do not look too pleased. At first I'm surprised, but then I know what's wrong—or what I think might be wrong. I suspect that he wants the cast to fight and act crazy and totally humiliate themselves in front of the camera—because that's probably what the viewers expect.

As the party continues and midnight draws closer, it looks like the director may get his way. Whether it's due to his suggestions or simply natural consequences, some of the cast appear to be 1) showing their true colors, 2) drinking too much, or 3) trying to get camera time. Because, once again, it feels like things are getting out of hand. Even some of the guys are acting feisty. Vince and Benjamin exchange words, although Juan helps to calm them down. And now Natasha is making some pretty malicious remarks to Paige—all related, it seems, to the fact that Benjamin keeps asking my sister to dance.

"Why is Natasha getting all nasty again?" I ask Avery while we're both in the bathroom at the same time. "I mean, I know she's Mia's friend, but Mia is MIA." I chortle at my own joke. "Seriously, does Natasha expect Benjamin to suddenly turn into a wallflower just because his girlfriend is gone? Or maybe she thinks he should go hold Mia's hand?"

Avery simply laughs. "You're not even close."

"What then? Is she showing off for the cameras?"

"Partially. But more than that, she's jealous of Paige." Avery drops her used towel into the bin. "Natasha probably assumed, with Mia out of the picture, it might be her big chance to go after Benjamin tonight."

"Nice friend."

Avery shrugs. "It's how the game is played." She pauses to freshen her lip gloss with one of the little disposable flasks from the basket on the vanity. "The director intentionally sets up the show so that girls outnumber guys. I think it's kind of like *The Bachelor*. You know, females vying for male attention. For some reason, probably because girls are über-competitive, it works."

"It works meaning more cattiness ..."

"That's what the viewers want. And most of the viewers are teenage girls. So what does that tell you?"

"That teenage girls are bloodthirsty."

Avery and I laugh and we both go back out. I watch as Avery rejoins Juan, heading for the dance floor with, it seems, no intentions of getting caught in the crossfire, which I must admit is both mature and admirable.

As I stand there watching the crowd, I wonder why teens are assumed to enjoy this kind of thing. It's like everyone thinks we thrive on conflict and chaos. Maybe some teens do. But I happen to think we have enough to struggle with simply to survive adolescence. Could it be possible that we don't need a steady diet of adolescent strife on reality television too? Then again, it's not like I'm much of an expert on this stuff since I hardly ever watch it. That irony doesn't escape me ... or how it must appear that I condone this stuff since I'm actually participating in not just one, but *two* teen reality shows. Again I have to ask myself, how did I end up here?

Somehow Paige and I make it until midnight with no missing hair, broken bones, or claw marks across our faces, and I am so relieved when we finally say our "Happy New Years," and I begin to entice Paige to go home.

"Come on, Cinderella," I tease her as I tug her away from

the dance floor. "I'm pretty sure our limo has turned into a pumpkin by now."

She makes a *call me* sign to Benjamin, then turns away and sighs. "Oh, Erin, you are such a party pooper."

"Aren't you curious about Mom?" I try. "I mean, tonight was her first date since Dad and—"

"Oh, man, Erin!" Paige is walking faster now. "I totally forgot about that. Let's hurry!"

Soon we're in the car. Fran has left, but there's a note saying that she'll call us in a day or two. And for some reason that just totally irks me. She was supposed to be the director, right? The responsible adult? Yet she just takes off like it's no big deal. What would've happened if there'd been a real problem? Even our camera guys are gone. Something about this just doesn't seem right, and I wonder if I should inform our mom. Not that I want to be the tattletale of the family. But, really, it seems weird.

Paige leans back in the seat and lets out a long sigh. "Benjamin is such a cool guy ..." She says this in a way that sounds too dreamy not to be taken seriously.

"Meaning what?" I ask her.

"Huh?" she looks at me as if she forgot I was there.

"Benjamin is such a cool guy—how? Like as an actor? As a friend? Or are you talking romance?"

She just smiles.

"Paige," I say with a warning tone. "He's still going with Mia, you know."

"I know ... but it sounds like he's trying to break up."

"Trying to break up means they're still a couple, right?"

"Oh, Erin, you can be such a buzzkill."

Whatever. I lean back into the seat, cross my arms over

my front, close my eyes, and pretend she's not there. Childish, maybe, but I can't believe she's treating me like this. Especially when I think of how I rescued her tonight, not just once, but twice. Some appreciation I get!

Mom appears to have gotten home just ahead of us. I can tell by the look on her face that she probably had fun tonight. If I'm not mistaken, there seem to be actual stars in her eyes. In fact, I think that both Paige and Mom are wearing the same expression.

"So … how was your date?" Paige asks as she kicks off her shoes.

"Very nice." Mom sits down on the sectional and sighs. "Much nicer than I expected."

"Who exactly is this Jim, Tim, Tom guy anyway?" I ask, suddenly feeling like my dad—and that is pretty weird. But he was the type to get directly to the point and ask the hard questions, probably because he was a journalist.

Mom just smiles. "His name is Jon. J-O-N."

"And he works with you?" I say.

"Not exactly. He's a producer for a morning program. I've known him for a while. Very nice man."

"So, what's he like, Mom?" Paige sits down beside her. "Tell me everything. What's he look like? How old is he? Did he kiss you?"

Mom actually giggles. For some reason, I don't think I can handle this much information. I mean, I realize Mom has every right to romance. She probably *needs* romance, but I'm just not ready to hear the details. Not yet.

"I'm tired," I tell them. "I think I'll call it a night."

"Happy New Year, Sweetie," Mom says happily.

"Happy New Year to you," I say in a voice that doesn't

sound nearly as hopeful as it should. And really, I think, as I remove my fancy dress and shoes and wash what now looks like way too much makeup from my face, what is going to make this a happy year? I won't be going back to school. I'm trapped into doing reality TV, which is feeling more and more like a moral compromise. I'm feeling slightly alienated by my best friend Mollie, since she even admitted being jealous. My mom and my sister are both acting like airheads. So, really, what about this new year is going to be happy? Of course, that could just be exhaustion talking. I hope so.

Chapter

11

"Good news," Paige announces on New Year's Day.

I look up from my Cheerios and brace myself.

"We're invited to Mia's birthday party on Saturday."

"Yeah, right." I stick my spoon in my cereal and shake my head.

"It's a surprise party," Paige continues.

"Yes, I'm sure Mia will be surprised if *we* show up. Try shocked, stunned, and speechless as she reaches for her pepper spray."

"Why should Mia act like that?" Mom's in the kitchen now, pouring herself some coffee.

"Because Paige is trying to steal her boyfriend," I say under my breath.

"Erin!" Paige gives me a wounded expression.

"Oh?" Mom looks curious.

"I'm not trying to steal him," Paige defends herself. "I can't help it if Benjamin likes me. Or even if I like him."

Mom looks at me. "So why would you accuse Paige of stealing Mia's boyfriend?"

I look down at my Cheerios, pressing my lips together. Really, why not just keep my mouth shut? Except that I was kind of under the impression that part of my job on the show was to help keep my sister from self-destructing.

"Erin?" Mom is waiting.

I look at Paige, who is giving me the evil eye — and suddenly I don't really care. "Benjamin is still seeing Mia," I say quietly. "It might just be me, but it seems kind of unethical to move in on a guy while he's still with someone else."

Mom frowns like she doesn't know how to respond.

"I'm not moving in on anyone." Paige holds her head high.

"That's probably not how Mia sees it," I say to her. "She seemed pretty mad at you last night. And not just because you criticized her dress either. She seemed pretty certain you were moving in on Benjamin too."

"Mia's just like that," Paige says lightly. "A little drama queen. If you ever watched *Malibu Beach*, you would know this."

"Right." I roll my eyes. "Well, her act was convincing, because I think if she'd had a gun in her hand it would've been pointed at your head."

"And this girl has invited you to her birthday party?" Mom looks understandably confused.

"I said it's a surprise party." Paige is getting irate. "Mia isn't the one doing the inviting."

"Who is?" I ask.

"I'm not sure."

"Her boyfriend perhaps?" I venture.

"Look, the invitation came by way of Fran. Someone emailed her. Probably Rod Spencer."

"The director of *Malibu Beach*?" Mom asks with mild interest.

"Maybe ..." Paige frowns at me like I just rained on her parade.

"So is this a working gig?" I ask.

"It's publicity, Erin," she tells me with exasperation.

"It's a setup." I finish the last bite of Cheerios, then take my bowl to the sink. "Do you know that they deliberately cast more girls on that show than guys?" I say to Mom. "Just so there'll be competition amongst the girls?"

Mom makes a small chuckle. "Somehow that doesn't surprise me."

"But it's not right." I run water in my bowl. "And I'll bet the only reason Rod Spencer is inviting us to Mia's party is to stir things up. He probably wants Paige and Mia to get into a great big hair-pulling catfight. Maybe it'll raise their ratings."

"Like I would do that." Paige looks indignant as she pours some juice.

"If Mia saw you and Benjamin together, you might not have a choice," I warn her.

"Will Fran and your camera crew be there?" Mom asks with a concerned brow.

"I don't know." Paige sets her juice glass down with a bang. "Does it really matter?"

"It might." Mom sits down at the breakfast bar and presses her lips together. "I'm not sure how I feel about you girls getting pulled into the whole *Malibu Beach* thing. I don't like what I hear about that show. I thought *On the Runway* was supposed to be different."

"It *is* different," Paige says in a pleading voice. "It's just that Helen is trying to give us some exposure. And *Malibu Beach* is like —"

"Like overexposure," I finish for her.

"No, I was going to say it's one of the most popular teen shows right now. The more we can appear on that, the better known we'll be."

"Yes." I set my bowl in the dishwasher, then turn around to look at my sister. "And you'll become known as that boy-friend-stealing blonde who got her hair pulled out and face scratched up by the Malibu Barbies as they rushed to the defense of poor Mia Renwick at her own birthday party." I pour myself a cup of coffee, shaking my head. "But you know what they say, bad publicity is better than no publicity."

"Shut up!"

"Paige Marie!" Mom looks even more concerned now.

"Sorry, Mom, but Erin just goes too far."

"Erin is actually making sense."

"Thanks, Mom." I smile to myself as I add cream to my coffee.

But when I turn around, I notice that Mom's frowning at me. "Except you could be a little diplomatic about it."

"I exhausted my diplomacy skills last night." Even as I say this, I'm starting to feel guilty. It's not like I really want to throw Paige under the bus.

"Don't you mean your judgmental skills?" Paige glares at me.

Feeling a mixture of remorse and irritation, I sit down across from my glowering sister and try to adjust my attitude. "Sorry, Paige," I say in a calm tone. "But I honestly don't see how crashing Mia's birthday—"

"We're not crashing. We're *invited!*"

"Well, I have an idea," Mom proclaims. "Or maybe it's an edict."

"An edict?" Paige's brow creases and I wonder if she needs a pocket dictionary.

"If you girls want to go to Mia Renwick's birthday party, there are a couple of things you'll have to—"

"Who said I want to go?" I protest.

"Listen to my edict, Erin."

So I just sip my coffee, listening as Mom explains that if we go, we have to go together, and we each have to take our own dates. "That way there will be no squabbling over boyfriends."

"But I don't want to take a date," Paige complains.

"Then don't go," Mom shoots back.

"Besides," Paige tries, "Fran didn't say we could bring anyone else with us. And there will be a list at the party."

"Then I'll just call Fran and tell her that you won't be going and why."

Paige groans. "This is crazy."

"Take it or leave it." Mom picks up her coffee and hums as she goes to her bedroom.

"Thanks a lot," Paige tells me after Mom's door closes. "This is all your fault."

"*My* fault? I don't even want to go to the stupid party."

Paige glares at me. "You *have* to go."

"As far as I know this is a free country." Then, like Mom, I pick up my coffee and go to my bedroom. Let Paige stew.

And Paige does stew. For the rest of the day, she totally ignores me. Then, on the next day, when crummy weather keeps us both indoors, she's still not talking. On Friday, the sun comes out and I decide to finally make a trip to the desert to shoot photos. Knowing my mom will throw a fit if I go alone, I call Lionel to come with me, but he's still in Tahoe. Then I try Mollie and she's not answering, which worries me.

Mollie is usually the one calling me about ten times a day, but lately she's been silent. I hope I haven't done anything to offend her. Finally, in desperation, and since he's left several messages, I try Blake.

"It's about time you returned my calls," he says pleasantly, but in a way that's supposed to make me feel bad.

"Sorry."

"I heard about your big New Year's Eve gig," he says with a little too much interest.

"Let me guess, Facebook?"

"Of course. And Mollie keeps me informed."

"Where is she, by the way? Do you know?"

"I think she and Tony went to the beach."

"Right." I tell him about needing someone to accompany me to the desert. "The light is perfect today and I want to—"

"So I'm like your escort? Do I get paid for this service?"

"Fine," I say quickly, "if you don't want to go—"

"No, Erin, I'm just jerking your chain. Don't be so touchy."

"Oh ... well, Paige has been jerking my chain too. I guess I am a little sensitive."

He begs me to spill the beans on Paige, but instead I remind him that we're burning daylight and promise to disclose more information once we're on the road. "I'll pick you up in about thirty minutes," I say, unsure whether I'll regret this.

To my surprise, Blake turns out to be a good companion on my fieldtrip. He's even helpful as I'm taking photos. Unlike Lionel, who gets caught up in his own shots and equipment, Blake is catering only to me. And I must admit that I find it rather disarming ... and sweet.

Of course, my payment for his attention is to tell him about the New Year's party and Paige and the whole Benjamin and Mia thing, as well as the invitation to Mia's surprise party, where we can only go if we take a date. "Not that I plan on going," I tell him quickly. "Honestly, it feels like an accident waiting to happen."

"I can see how it could get a little explosive." He chuckles. "But that's what *Malibu Beach* is about. They love their fireworks."

"Tell me about it." I'm dropping him at his house now. He lives in a really swanky neighborhood about twenty minutes away, not too different from where we lived before our dad died. "Thanks for your help."

"And, don't forget, I got first dibs if you change your mind about Mia's birthday party tomorrow," he reminds me as he closes the door to my Jeep.

"Yeah, right." I roll my eyes. "See ya!"

I'm barely home and it's apparent that all is forgiven as my sister is speaking to me again. "How was the desert?" she asks pleasantly.

"Good," I tell her as I put down my bags and head to the fridge for some ice water.

"Good."

I can tell by the tone of her voice that she wants something. And it doesn't take a mind reader to guess what it is.

"So …" She smiles sweetly. "I talked to Fran today."

"Right." I take another swig of water.

"And she really wants to see us go to that party."

"To surprise Mia?"

Paige bites her bottom lip.

"Doesn't that seem mean to you?" I ask her. "I mean, how would you feel if it was reversed? What if it was your birthday and your boyfriend and—"

"I'm not going there to get Benjamin," she shoots back at me.

"But it—"

"I already invited Addison to go with me."

"Did you mention to Addison how you feel about Benjamin?"

She waves her hand. "Oh, I was just crushing on Benjamin. You know that, Erin. It's silly, really. Like, he's the big celeb and it was fun to catch his eye. I know it's not anything more than that. And to be fair, you know he's just playing me for his own publicity too. That's all it is."

I'm sure the skepticism is written all over my face as I refill my glass.

"Anyway, you might be interested to hear what Fran said about you."

"Fran said something about me?"

"Just that you were brilliant."

"Fran said I was brilliant?"

Paige nods firmly. "She looked over the film from the New Year's party and she really liked how you handled things. When I told her it was your idea to do the interview thing outside of the party, she said you were brilliant."

I try not to feel too impressed with myself.

"And ... she really wants us to go to Mia's party."

"Yeah, you already mentioned that."

"So, come on, Erin, will you do this for me?" She smiles hopefully. "And for our show?"

"Well, I do have a volunteer to escort me," I confess.

"Great!" She gives me a high five. "Who?"

"Blake."

Her expression turns sober, and she's probably wondering

if I'm making a bad move. "But … I thought he was seeing that Sonya chick."

"He was. But he broke up with her before Christmas and now he keeps telling me that I'm the only one, that he's always loved me, and stuff like that." I shake my head as if I'm still not convinced.

"Wow, do you believe him?"

"I don't know." I shrug. "But just because he'll be my date to Mia's party doesn't mean that we're back together, right? I mean, you and Addison aren't a real couple either."

"No way. This is just show biz, baby." She laughs. "And, don't worry, Addison knows that up front."

"If you really think it'll help our show, I guess I'm willing. Not eager," I remind her, "but willing."

"It's the same deal as the last party. We need to get to the studio by one tomorrow to turn in our New Year's outfits and pick up new ones."

"Another formal party?" I groan.

"No, you're in luck. This is more of a beach party. But you know how those *Malibu Beach* girls are. They never go slumming. And neither can we."

"Especially you … with your fashion reputation." I realize just how much I don't envy her role. What a relief that no one's judging my sense of style.

"The stakes continue to rise." Paige is totally nonchalant, like this is nothing more than just playing Barbies. And maybe that's not too far off—Malibu Barbies. I can't help but think about our childhood Barbies, and how it seems Paige was made for this.

I retreat to my room, trying to decide whether or not I really want to call Blake. I know he'll probably be ecstatic at the possibility of meeting the cast of the hottest teen reality show, and I realize I sort of promised him. And yet, I'm not sure. Maybe Lionel would be a better choice.

I turn on my computer to download my desert photos, and I have this weird sense of relief that Paige and I are going to Mia's party. Of course, it's not that I'm glad about the silly surprise party. But I am happy that Paige and I are talking again. She may be a sometimes-intolerable fashion freak, but she's still my sister.

Chapter 12

"*Seriously?*" *Blake asks me again*.

"No. I'm lying," I say sarcastically.

"I really get to be on *Malibu Beach*?"

"I can't believe you're this excited, Blake." I feel guilty for having called Lionel first—even after I'd promised Blake that he'd get the chance. I guess I just had cold feet.

"Hey, what can I say? I think it sounds like fun. And you know how much Katie loves that show. She'll go nuts when she hears about this."

"How is little Katie anyway?"

"'Little Katie' is probably taller than you now. She just turned thirteen last month and she's gotten so mouthy, my mom's considering military school for her next year." He pauses. "I really get to be on *Malibu Beach* with you, huh?"

"I can't promise that you'll make it on the air. They film almost everything that goes on, but most of it ends up getting cut. I'm actually hoping that anything I'm in will be cut."

"Why?"

Why? How do I begin to explain why? We dated for a long time. Shouldn't he know why? "Because—"

"Wait. Let me guess. Because you're more comfortable behind the camera than in front of it."

"Right." I guess Blake does still get me.

"And I can respect that, Erin. But I happen to think you're a beautiful girl and I wish you—"

"Yeah, yeah," I cut him off. "You don't need to butter me up. You're invited to the party already. But I do want to be straight with you about something, okay?"

"Okay." I imagine he's bracing for another one of my spiels.

"This isn't a real date."

"Meaning I'm still on probation?"

"Not probation ..." I don't like the way he puts it, but I can't help but think he's actually kind of spot-on.

"Whatever."

"It's the same deal as when you went to the desert with me yesterday. We're *friends*, Blake. For now that's all. If my inviting you to this party makes you think we're dating again, I'll just have to—"

"I get it, Erin." He sounds a little dejected. "And that's fine."

"Good. So here are the details. You'll come over here at seven so that you can ride with us in the limo. Our director, Fran, will be riding with us and she'll give you and Addison some tips. Then we'll all get wired for sound. When we get out of the limo, the fun begins."

"So what do I wear? How do I act? Anything I should know?" He sounds like a little kid on Christmas morning and I can't help but think it's kind of cute.

"Maybe I should have Paige call you. She's the expert

when it comes to how to dress. As far as how to act, they'll all tell you to just be yourself, only more so."

"More so?"

"I'm not saying that's a good idea. I think the directors just like to hype things up, you know, to make the show more sensational."

"So there's no script?"

"It's reality TV."

"I know, but sometimes it almost seems like those shows are scripted, like the kids are acting."

I think back to my conversation with Avery. "Well, sometimes they're staged, but not really scripted." Suddenly I'm wondering if Blake will want to act too. After all, he was into drama in high school. He still helps out with skits for our youth group sometimes. In a way, he's a bit of a ham.

"So can you have Paige call me?" he asks with slight hesitation. "For, uh, some fashion advice?"

I try not to laugh as I remember how this guy takes style more seriously than I do. "Sure," I tell him. "But right now, Paige and I need to go to the studio to get our own outfits. My guess is that Paige will be better able to advise you after she knows what she's wearing. I mean, she wouldn't want anyone to upstage her."

He chuckles. "No worries there."

"See you at seven then."

"Can't wait."

As I hang up I have mixed feelings. On one hand, it's hard not to start falling for this guy again. Blake is a lot of fun and he still really seems to care about me. On the other hand, I still question his timing ... and his motives. And I wonder if it's possible that he broke up with Sonya, and started pursuing me again, simply because of the TV deal. Blake was always the one who wanted an acting career. And even though his dad talked him into more traditional education, I remember how he really wanted to do the UCLA program in film and TV.

I put these concerns behind me as Paige and I head over to the studio.

"My goal is to win Mia over," Paige tells me as she stops for a light. "I want to give her a really cool birthday present. I just don't know what it should be."

"How about a written promise to stay away from her boyfriend," I tease.

"Give me a break."

"Well, I'm sure Mia will be relieved to see you brought your own date tonight." I point to the green light. "I actually think that was pretty brilliant of Mom to suggest that."

"So are you saying I shouldn't even look at Benjamin? I mean, what if he says hi? Am I supposed to ignore him?"

"I'm sure you'll figure it out."

"Fine. Back to Mia's birthday present." Paige drums her fingers on the steering wheel as she waits for the next light. "What would make her trust me?"

"I don't think you can *make* anyone trust you, Paige."

"You know what I mean. What would get to her ... in a good way?"

"What kind of gift would get to you?" I ask.

Paige gets a thoughtful look. "Diamonds."

I laugh. "Well, sorry, but you can't afford diamonds."

"True. But maybe the show can afford something. This is for publicity, right? Why can't we, on behalf of *On the Runway*, give Mia something special?"

"I guess you can ask Fran."

"Like a real Badgley Mischka dress!"

"I don't know … what if Mia got offended, like you were trying to remind her that she'd worn a fake?"

"Good point. But maybe some other hot designer. Fran says that she's been getting all kinds of cool stuff from designers who want a little publicity."

And so, not only do Paige and I pick up our outfits—which still seem overly dressy for a real beach party, but Fran assures us are "perfect"—we also leave with a birthday present for Mia. Fran thought it was a great idea, especially in light of the upcoming fashion show that Mia is helping to organize. "We need to stay on her good list," Fran reminded Paige. And after some serious perusing, they finally decided on a size four Vera Wang dress in a soft periwinkle color that Paige says will be stunning on Mia. I just hope it doesn't blow up in our faces.

"Don't forget to call Blake," I remind Paige when we get home.

"Oh, that's right. Fashion direction." She pauses to study me. "You decided on the Ralph Lauren dress, right? The nautical one?"

"Yeah. You called it my little sailor dress, remember?"

"It looked great on you."

"Well, at least it was comfortable."

She nods. "Okay, I know just what Blake can wear. We'll keep it sweet and simple. Khakis, a pale-blue-and-white-striped oxford shirt—preferably Ralph Lauren—and topsiders."

I smile like I care, then go to my room, where I'd like to take a fashion break and print out some of the desert photos I took yesterday. But I've barely started when Lionel calls. "Hey, I saw you called a couple times," he says. "What's up?"

I quickly explain my need for a date, and before I can tell him that I already asked Blake, he is volunteering. "I should be home by five," he tells me. "Give me an hour and I can be—"

"Sorry," I interrupt. "I was kind of desperate, you know, so I called Blake."

"Blake?" His voice sounds stiff.

"I know that probably seems pretty random."

"A little." He sounds slightly hurt.

"Well . . . when you couldn't go to the desert with me, and I knew my mom would be mad if I went alone, and Mollie wasn't around, well, I kind of asked Blake to go. And then when you weren't around for the party, I just—"

"You don't have to explain, Erin." He sounds formal.

"I know. But you're my friend."

"Right. And I'm sorry I wasn't there for you."

"It's okay!"

"And I hope you're not getting in over your head with Blake."

Part of me wants to question what he means by this, but another part says *let it go*. And anyway, I can pretty much guess what he means. "Sorry about the miscommunication," I say. Then to change the subject I ask him about his ski trip, but he tells me that he's just getting into traffic and probably shouldn't be on the phone, and so we hang up. And then I feel guilty, but I'm not even sure why.

"You guys look great," Fran says as the four of us pile into the limo—a real limo this time.

"Thanks," Paige tells her. "With Erin and Blake I was going for more of a preppy-ingénue look. Sort of yacht club. And

Addison and I are more like the islands … maybe Jamaica, don't you think?"

"This is why we love you, Paige." Fran nods approvingly at Addison's white shirt, linen pants, and sandals. The perfect complement to Paige's off-white dress with embroidered birds and flowers. When she had first held this dress up on a hanger, I thought she was kidding. But when I saw it on her, I knew it was perfect. And fortunately, the weather has been dry and unseasonably warm today, just right for a beach party. If this really were a party. I have to keep reminding myself that it's not—it's work. As if to drive that point home, we begin wiring ourselves for sound.

"Our camera crew won't be allowed access within the party," Fran tells us as we fiddle with our mics and wires. "But like the other night, you'll get as much time with them as you want outside of the party. Unfortunately, they probably won't want you hanging outside though, since this is supposedly a surprise party." She laughs. "Like Mia doesn't know."

"Does Mia know *we're* coming?" I ask.

Fran just shrugs. "Hard to say. It was their producer who extended the invitation. Anyway, all four of your names should be on the list. The best plan is probably to head in there and then, later on, see if you can lure anyone outside for the sake of our cameras." She looks to me. "You did a great job with that last time, Erin."

"Most of them were more than willing once they realized they might be seen on our show too," I tell her.

Next, Fran preps the guys for what's in store, and tells them to just be themselves. "Don't let those kids intimidate you. But don't be camera hogs either." She chuckles. "Just because you're at a *Malibu Beach* party does not mean you're going to be instant stars. Most likely you'll end up on the cutting-room floor."

Suddenly it's time to get out and I'm feeling seriously nervous. Despite Paige's noble plan to win Mia over, I realize that tonight's "party" could be even more challenging than the last one.

"Have a good time," Fran says as we get out of the limo.

"This is so fun," Blake tells me as he takes my arm.

I lower my voice, shielding my mic. "Oh, and just FYI— there's a lot of drinking at these parties ..."

He shrugs. "I don't plan to get caught up in that." As the camera crew comes closer, he puts on his Hollywood smile. "But I don't mind getting caught by the cameras."

I consider warning him that with Paige leading the way, there's not much chance the cameras will be interested in us. But, hey, why spoil his fun? I must admit that it's kind of reassuring to have him with me tonight. And even if he's just using me as his opportunity to grab fifteen minutes of fame (more like fifteen seconds, and that's if he's lucky) I suppose I'm kind of using him too, but it's in a friendly way ... I think.

Chapter
13

We give our names to security at the front door and enter the house with Paige and Addison leading the way. This house isn't as enormous as the New Year's location, but it's equally impressive. We've been told to go inside since the house is also the entryway to the beach party, which is actually contained within a cordoned-off area of the beach with even more security posted all around. Apparently anything regarding the *Malibu Beach* show is a high security risk. Whether it's a fear of being mobbed by crazed fans or mugged by enraged parents sick of the influence of teen reality shows is anyone's guess.

We're not even clear through the house yet, and it's plain to see that we've made this "surprise" party even more surprising.

"What are *they* doing here?" Natasha says loudly enough for everyone, including a couple of camera guys, to hear. She's standing near the back doors with a cluster of other girls and clearly not thrilled to see us.

"Hey, everyone," Paige calls out in a friendly voice. "Before you start stoning us, let me say that we come in peace. And, just so you know, we *were* invited."

"Don't mind Natasha," Brogan tells Paige. "She's just mad because she was rejected for yet another modeling gig."

"Shut up!" Natasha snaps at her friend. The cameras are focusing in on this little spat.

Then, with a beautifully wrapped present in hand, Paige just shakes her head. "That totally floors me."

Natasha narrows her eyes. "Yeah, I'll bet it does."

"Seriously." Paige looks evenly at Natasha now. "You really have the right look going on to model professionally, Natasha. Maybe you're just talking to the wrong people. I can so imagine you on a New York runway."

Natasha softens a bit. "Really?"

"Absolutely." Paige nods firmly. "And you guys know me. I'm honest about anything related to fashion—even if I do step on toes."

Natasha almost smiles now. "I won't ask for your opinion on my dress tonight."

Paige looks down at the yellow dress and smiles. "It's lovely."

"What?" Natasha peers closer at Paige. "Are you really Paige Forrester, the fashion fiend?"

Paige just laughs. "Hey, it's a nice dress. What can I say? Michael Kors. Right?"

Natasha nods with a stunned expression.

Then Paige introduces both Addison and Blake to the girls. Naturally, she can remember everyone's names. "We were told it was okay to bring dates tonight." She slips her arm behind Addison, smiling into his face as if he's her main man, which is so not true. I try hard not to roll my eyes.

"That might make *some* girls happier." Brogan jerks her thumb toward the back doors leading to the beach. "The plan is to have everyone outside and to turn the lights off when we get the signal that Mia is here."

"Which should be in about five minutes," Avery warns.

"And food and drinks are out there," Natasha adds. "We won't start the music until Mia arrives. We want her to be surprised."

"You mean she really doesn't know about this party?" I ask.

Avery laughs. "Well, of course she knows we're shooting a show. But no one told her that it was a show about her *surprise* party."

"Won't she guess by the security outside that something's going on?" I ask.

"The camera guys in front are supposed to lay low," Brogan explains. "We have a guy posted at the end of the street who's supposed to call as soon as Mia and Benjamin are spotted."

"But Mia probably already knows what's up," Natasha tells us. "It's hard to keep secrets in this town."

"Or from Mia," Avery says, "The girl's totally wired. If she's not twittering, TMing, checking Facebook or email, she's probably just on the phone. Not much slips past her."

I wonder if that includes her boyfriend. But I don't say this out loud. "Want to go outside?" I ask Blake.

"Sure." He reminds me of a kid in a candy store. It's like his eyes are glittering—almost as much as some of the jewelry these girls are wearing. And I can tell he's trying to look good for the cameras, not that they seem to care. We are definitely not the focus here. And, even though Blake and I don't quite fit in (the other girls' dresses are far more sophisticated and revealing than mine), I don't even care. It's almost as if I don't *want* to fit in. Maybe that's just stubbornness on my part. Or an attempt to preserve my personal identity.

Once we're outside, I do try to be friendly. I introduce Blake to some of the guys that I remember from before, including Juan and Vince. We are just getting sodas when the lights suddenly go off and someone near the door makes a loud shushing sound.

Before long, Mia and Benjamin arrive—the lights go on and everyone shouts, *"Surprise! Happy Birthday!"* Mia feigns shock and the party continues merrily along. That is, until Mia spots Paige. Then it's as if the whole place goes silent and I expect to hear that weird music—the kind they play in old westerns at high noon when gunfighters meet in the center of the town.

"Paige?" Mia says in a voice that I'm sure she wants to sound normal. "I didn't expect to see you here tonight."

"Happy Birthday," Paige says cheerfully. "You look absolutely beautiful."

"Uh-huh ..." Mia glances over at Benjamin and he looks slightly uncomfortable, as if he's as surprised by this as she is.

"I'd like you to meet my date," Paige says quickly, introducing them to Addison like he's her trophy. "Your producer invited us and this time he allowed us to bring our own dates," she jokes.

"Well, isn't that nice." Mia is smiling, but her eyes are like ice.

"And I brought you something," Paige continues. I can tell she's getting nervous, maybe wondering if this wasn't such a great idea after all.

"Good idea," Natasha says quickly. "Why don't you open your presents now, Mia." She nods to Avery and some others. "Want to help bring the gifts in for her?"

Mia looks uncertain, but she nods. "Sure, okay."

Paige goes with other girls, returning with her present in hand. It's the largest one there and by far the prettiest, but it sits conspicuously off to one side as Natasha starts handing Mia the other presents. And Mia opens them with what seems polite interest. A couple of spa certificates, some perfume—which she says is her favorite, a large basket of bath products, some fancy chocolates, and a charm bracelet from Benjamin that doesn't really seem to hit the mark. I wonder if she expected a ring instead. Finally she is done, except for the package that Paige has picked up and is now holding out toward Mia.

"Last but hopefully not least," Paige says as she hands the box to Mia. "It's actually from our show, *On the Runway*, but I picked it out especially for you."

Mia cautiously unties the lush satin ribbon and opens the box, removing layers of pink tissue paper before finally lifting out the dress.

"It's from Vera Wang's line," Paige gushes. "We got a sneak preview for the show, but when I saw that color, I knew it would look fabulous on you. She'll have one similar to it for New York Fashion Week, but she was hoping we'd use it on our show first."

"Really?" Mia looks truly surprised.

"And we thought you might even want to wear it for your benefit show," Paige says hopefully. "Or not. I mean, it's your dress to do with as you like. But I think it's going to look great on you."

Natasha comes over to examine the garment. "This dress is *really nice*."

"And it's not a knockoff," Brogan says with a twinkle in her eyes.

"Absolutely not," Paige assures them. "It's the real deal. Happy birthday, Mia!"

Mia looks stunned. "Thanks, Paige."

Paige takes this little love fest even further and reaches down to hug Mia. "Bygones?"

Mia just nods.

I exchange glances with Blake, but I can tell he's as impressed as I am. Seriously, how does my sister do it? I have no doubts that if Mia had mafia relatives, she would've had a hit out on Paige. Now they're acting like best friends. Maybe my sister should give up being a fashion advisor and just teach charm school, as I'm sure she could make millions.

The party continues with no big incidents. Not that this makes the *Malibu Beach* camera crew happy. But the *On the Runway* crew seems pleased when Paige and I lure a number of cast members outside to do some quick interviews and "fashion chats," as Paige is calling them. Even Mia, at her friends' encouragement, tries on the Vera Wang dress then goes out to do a "birthday" interview with Paige while wearing it. Really, I do not know how this evening could've gone much better. And for the whole night, Paige keeps a safe distance from Benjamin. By the time we leave, Mia and Paige, once again, exchange air kisses.

"And I'll see you next week for your fashion show," Paige reminds Mia.

"Thanks for coming tonight," Mia calls happily.

As we drive home, I relay the amazing story of Paige's reconciliation with Mia to Fran. And yet Fran isn't even surprised. "That's why Helen Hudson picked your sister," she says as if it should be obvious. "Paige Forrester's got the magic touch."

Paige is beaming at this high praise and suddenly I'm worried it might all go to her head, and there'll be no living with her if that happens. Still, I must admit I admire her diplomacy skills. And there might be a thing or two she could teach me.

Chapter
14

Before I got a chance to sign up as the latest member of the Paige Forrester fan club, and trust me, there is one, my sister did something that seriously tipped her halo. Not that she's ever been much of an angel. Although some people think her golden hair, blue eyes, and sweet smile are angelic, I know better. And I should've known better than to think that Paige would continue along the high road when it came to Benjamin Kross.

"You're doing what?" I ask, just two days after her Oscar-worthy performance as Miss Congeniality at Mia's birthday party.

"Don't act like I'm a criminal, Erin." I've cornered her in the bathroom. Not that she cares since she's only doing her makeup.

"I just want to make sure I heard you right. Did you just say that you're going out with Benjamin tonight?"

"So?" She puts the mascara lid back on and blinks innocently.

"*So?*" I stare at her. How can she possibly be so dense?

"What about Mia? What about your little spiel at her birthday? All that bygones and burying the hatchet? Was that just an act?"

She shrugs as she opens her lip gloss and refocuses her attention to the mirror.

"It was?" I want to shake her. "Really? *Just an act?*"

"No ... not exactly. I mean, yes, I did want to smooth things over for the sake of the fashion show on Saturday. I couldn't just let that fall apart, could I? Our show is supposed to be there, remember? How do we do that if Mia won't speak to me?"

"Yes!" I point my forefinger up, as in *ah-hah!* "That's my question too—how do we cover the fashion show if Mia is enraged at you for going out with her boyfriend?"

"He's not her boyfriend." She holds her blush brush in the air like she's going to duel my forefinger with it.

"Since when?"

"Well, they haven't *officially* broken up ... I mean on the show. But it's over."

"Says who?" I put my finger down and wait as she dusts a bit of blush on her cheeks.

"Benjamin."

"But what about Mia?"

"You know, Erin, it seems like you're more concerned about poor Mia Renwick than you are for your own sister."

"Oh, don't worry," I say. "I'm concerned about you too." I follow her out into the living room. It's obvious my opinion means nothing to her.

She gives me a photo-worthy smile as she reaches for her purse. "Don't be. I'm perfectly capable of taking care of myself, little sister."

"Fine," I snap at her. "And if *On the Runway* falls by the roadside, I won't be concerned about that either."

"Stop being such a drama queen."

I shake my head and go back to my room, firmly closing the door behind me. I cannot believe she's the one calling *me* a drama queen. And as I sit on my bed, I tell myself that I couldn't care less. Why should I care? Paige can marry Benjamin if she wants. Our show can be cancelled. So what? I don't want to do a show with Paige anyway . . . remember?

I am getting increasingly frustrated that I gave up my spot in the film and TV program at UCLA in order to participate in a reality show that may never become reality. That is, if my sister keeps acting like a total idiot. I wonder if it's too late to register for some classes for next term.

"Erin?" I hear my mom calling and think, yes, maybe this is the answer. Mom can talk some sense into my senseless sister. I find her in the kitchen putting away groceries, but before I can launch into my Paige complaints, Mom is telling me that she's invited Jon to dinner.

"Tomorrow night," she continues. "I want both you girls to be here. We'll eat at about seven thirty."

"Sounds like a big deal," I say with a smile as I put the lettuce in the vegetable bin. "Are you and Jon getting serious?"

Mom laughs. "Oh, I wouldn't call it serious. But I do think it's time he met you and Paige. I also thought it might be fun for all of us to watch *Malibu Beach* together. You know, you girls might actually be on it this week."

"Maybe Paige. I'm sure I ended up on the cutting-room floor." I put the orange juice in the fridge. "But speaking of Paige . . . I still can't believe she's dating Benjamin."

"Yes, isn't that amazing?"

"*Amazing?*" I close the door and turn to Mom. "Are you nuts?"

"Why?" Mom gives me a blank look.

"*Why?* Because Benjamin hasn't even broken up with Mia yet. Because our show is supposed to be covering Mia's big fashion show in a few days." I shove a container of oatmeal into the cabinet. "Because Paige made Mia believe they were friends. Because it's just wrong." I slam the cabinet door too loudly. "*That's why!*"

"You sound angry." Mom is peering at me now, like I'm the one with the problem here.

"I'm just frustrated, I guess." My hands ball into fists as I consider how I dropped out of film school—a program that's not easy to get into—just to help Paige succeed with *On the Runway*, and this is how she thanks me. "I mean, I'm giving up a lot for Paige's stupid show and now she's putting everything at risk for a stupid boy. How fair is that?"

Mom seems to consider this. "Do you think you could be blowing this out of proportion?"

"Mom, you haven't been around those kids. Do you even watch *Malibu Beach?*"

"Well, no . . ."

"Well, maybe you should. It gets pretty brutal. And if Mia finds out that Paige is dating Benjamin behind her back, I sure don't want to be at Mia's big fashion show to see what she and her friends do to get even then."

"Okay, let's back up the truck, Erin. Now did you say that Benjamin and Mia are still dating?"

"Yes."

"But Paige told me they broke up."

"Benjamin might want to break up, but it's not official. I

guess he thinks he needs to do it on the show." I shake my head. "How mean is that?"

"Probably raises ratings."

"Whatever. Anyway, do you think it's right for Paige to be dating a guy who's still going out with another girl?"

Mom gets a thoughtful look. "No, of course not. But at the same time, I can't tell Paige what to do, can I?"

"You could advise her against it. Not that she'll listen." I look over to Paige's partially closed bedroom door and wonder if she's listening to us right now.

"I can tell her what I think," Mom says quietly. "But she'll have to make up her mind about it."

"I can hear you guys," Paige says as she comes out looking like she's getting ready to pose for the cover of *Elle*. "And I appreciate your concern, but you just don't understand."

"Why don't you help us then," Mom tells her. "Tell us why you think it's wise to date Benjamin while he's still technically going with another girl."

"Because it's only technically. *Malibu Beach* is a *TV show*," she tells us as if we've both been living underground for the past several decades. "The kids on the show are paid to make things look edgy and real and complicated. And, like Benjamin said, the director is going to get a lot of mileage out of the breakup. Benjamin said they're planning to use it to promote that episode — *the breakup episode. Get it?"

"So . . . you're saying that Benjamin is only acting?"

"Exactly!" Paige puts the strap of her Gucci purse over her shoulder and glances at her watch. "And now, if you'll excuse me, I have to go."

"Isn't Benjamin picking you up?" Mom asks with a creased brow.

"No, we're meeting." Paige gets a sneaky look. "A clandestine meeting, to make sure no paparazzi see us."

"So if there's no problem," I inject, "why worry about paparazzi?"

"It's all about timing, little sister. We don't want to tip our hand too soon."

"Then why not just wait," I ask. "Go out with Benjamin after the big breakup episode airs."

She looks shocked. "Are you kidding?"

I just shake my head no.

"That's like forever. Benjamin and I want to be together *now*, Erin. And, trust me, we know what we're doing." Paige puts on an oversized pair of Gucci sunglasses she has somehow managed to afford, like she thinks that's some clever disguise. "No one will know."

"Right." I roll my eyes and wonder where my sister was when God was handing out common sense — probably gazing at herself in a mirror.

"Later," Paige chirps at us as she goes her merry way.

"See," I tell Mom after the front door closes. "She's oblivious. And she's putting our show in jeopardy. I wonder what Helen Hudson would say if she knew."

"Oh, Erin," Mom says calmly. "I'm sure your sister is more concerned over putting your show at risk than you are. *On the Runway* means a lot to her. And, if anything, I'm guessing Helen Hudson would see this as a fantastic publicity opportunity. The star of *On the Runway* dating the star of *Malibu Beach* — just the kind of thing tabloids love. And, for all we know, Mia Renwick might simply be acting too. Maybe she's not really into Benjamin as much as you think."

"Maybe not. But I wouldn't bet on it." I let out a long sigh as I trek back to my room. Mom's probably right. Tabloids *will* love this. And maybe Helen Hudson and Fran will love it too. Maybe I'm the crazy person here. It figures.

In need of consolation, I call Mollie, but once again, she doesn't answer. And I check my phone and see it's been ages since she's called me. That makes me wonder: Is she really this busy or is she snubbing me? I decide to check in with Blake.

"Hey, Erin," he says cheerfully. "How's it going?"

"Hey. Have you seen Tony or Mollie lately?"

"Well, I missed seeing them at fellowship group on Saturday night," he begins slowly, "but that's because I was with you at that birthday party. Then I slept in the next morning and didn't make it to church."

"Neither did I," I admit.

"Hey," he says suddenly. "It's not too late to make the midweek service."

"That's right." I run my fingers through my hair.

"Want to go?"

"Maybe I need to go."

"How about I pick you up?"

"Sounds good." Maybe Mollie and Tony will be there.

"See ya at seven."

As I get ready for church, I realize that I have really been missing fellowship. Between being at my grandmother's during the holidays, the New Year's party, and the birthday party, I've only been to church about once in the past several weeks. And even though I try to read my Bible somewhat regularly, and I pray whenever I feel like it, I feel pretty spiritually dry at the moment.

We arrive a few minutes late, but soon we're seated and the rich sound of the worship band playing and singing the words to those familiar songs feels like medicine to me. And before long I'm feeling hopeful and positive, and by the end of the service, which happens to be about forgiveness, I even manage to forgive my sister. Do I agree with what she's doing? No. But at least I won't let it build a wall between us. Because whether Paige knows it or not, she needs me. And maybe I need her too.

After church, we mill around and visit with some friends, but I don't see Mollie and Tony anywhere. Not that this is so unusual since they don't always go to midweek service, but I had hoped to see Mollie tonight.

"Hey, Erin," Lionel comes over to join us, eyeing Blake curiously. "Hey, Blake. What's up?"

"Not much," I tell him, suddenly feeling uncomfortable but not quite knowing why. I mean, Lionel's been a good friend, but it's not like we've ever been a couple. And yet I get the feeling that he's not happy to see me with Blake.

"How was the birthday party?" he asks.

"It actually went pretty well," I tell him with a smile. "Thanks for asking."

"It was fun," Blake adds. "In a crazy Hollywood sort of way. My little sister is telling all her friends that I'm going to be on the show now, but I kind of doubt that I'll make the cut."

"Maybe you should be glad for that," Lionel tells him.

I want to ask Lionel what he means by that, but I suspect I already know. I think Lionel thinks this whole reality TV business is kind of shallow and silly . . . and a waste of time . . . and not very spiritual. I totally agree.

We tell Lionel good-bye and head out, but I can't help but feel somewhat discouraged, or maybe I'm offended, by his attitude. And this bugs me on two levels. First of all, I wonder why I should be bothered that he looks down his nose on reality TV shows. Wasn't that my exact attitude from the start? Secondly, I'm disturbed that I'm feeling compromised—like I should defend my involvement with *On the Runway*. All this is seriously bumming me out, and I was actually feeling pretty good after the worship service.

"You okay?" Blake asks as he's driving away from the church.

"Yeah ... fine."

"You just got kind of quiet. You seemed happy during church, and now you seem down again."

"I was happy in church," I admit. "Thanks for asking me to go with you tonight. I needed it even more than I realized."

"Me too."

"The truth is, I probably need it more than ever now that I'm doing the show with Paige ... assuming we're still doing it, that is."

"Assuming?" Blake glances curiously at me.

I tell him about Paige and Benjamin. And it's a relief that his reaction is similar to mine. "Wow," he says, "I wouldn't want to be in Paige's shoes when Mia finds out about this. I noticed the look in that girl's eyes when she first saw Paige at her party. Paige was great at smoothing things over, but Mia does not seem like the kind of girl to take something like this lying down."

"That's exactly what I think."

"I just hope Paige knows what she's doing."

"I doubt that." I sigh. "In fact, maybe it would be a good thing if our show fell apart—I mean, if Paige messes it up so badly that we lose this opportunity."

"A *good* thing?" He frowns. "Why?"

"I don't know ... I'm just thinking maybe being on a show like that and being a Christian aren't really compatible"

"I can't believe you'd say something like that." Blake looks seriously disappointed. "Remember how we used to talk, Erin, how we'd say that Christians need to get involved in the entertainment industry to show that life can be lived differently than the way we so often see it being portrayed on shows, say, like *Malibu Beach*."

"I know ..."

"And I watch my little sister just drinking that *Malibu* stuff in like it's the gospel. Katie sometimes even starts acting like Mia Renwick—as if she thinks she's this entitled princess too. And then I feel even more strongly about the need for Christians to get involved. In fact, I'm considering switching schools and changing majors after this term ends, or maybe in the fall. I'm not sure yet. But, more than ever, I see the need for Christians to have an influence in film and TV, and I'm sorry I caved to my dad about school."

"Really?"

He nods. "It made sense at first. You know how it is here in LA, everyone and their great-aunt Mary wants to be in the entertainment industry, and there's only so much room. But to just give up? I don't know. I guess I need to pray about this whole thing. But seeing the opportunity that you have, Erin. Man, it just gives me hope, you know?"

"I guess so," I'm surprised by how much Blake is encouraging me. "To be honest, I haven't exactly been looking at it from that angle. I guess I've been pretty self-centered lately. Ironic since I keep telling myself that it's Paige who's self-absorbed. Seriously, I think it's really me."

"How so?"

"Like I keep worrying about how this show is going to affect me and my future. Or how things like appearing on *Malibu Beach* makes me uncomfortable. Plus, I find myself judging people like Mia and her friends. It's like I'm looking at this whole thing backward."

"Maybe so."

"I should be asking myself: How can God use me? How can I make a difference? How can I be a light in what seems a pretty dark place?"

"Yes!" He pounds his hand on the steering wheel. *"That's it!"*

"Wow, Blake." I turn and smile at him. "It's like I'm still in church. Great sermon. Thank you!"

"Hey, you're the one doing the preaching, sister."

I laugh and nod. "I guess so. But you must've been giving me the right prompts."

"I'll tell you what, Erin."

"What?"

"I'm going to be praying for you. And I'll ask the others in our fellowship group to pray too. I know you and Paige are going to be traveling and covering things and you might not make it to church as much as you used to. But you will have a bunch of brothers and sisters praying for you, okay?"

"Thanks. I really appreciate that. And I appreciate your friendship too," I admit.

"Hey, does that mean I'm off of probation now?"

I laugh. "It's just that I need a friend more than I need a boyfriend at the moment. Okay?"

"Okay." He nods. "But when you get to that needing a boyfriend place, you'll keep me on the list, right?"

"Absolutely."

"High on the list?"

"It's such a great long list," I tease.

"But Lionel's on it . . . isn't he?"

"Why would you say that?"

"Because I can tell he *wants* to be on it."

"Oh . . ." I just shrug. "Well, like I said, I'm not in the market for a boyfriend. But the truth is, you've been a really good friend lately—maybe even my best friend."

"Cool." He grins. "I can live with that. At least for now."

"Great. So can I." Okay, I feel a tiny bit guilty for Mollie's sake because she really is my best friend. At least I thought she was. But, seriously, she's not been much of a friend recently.

Chapter

15

"*Do we need five place settings?*" *I'm help-*ing Mom get ready for her big dinner with Jon tonight. But she's set a stack of five plates on the breakfast bar.

"Yes, didn't you know that Benjamin is joining us too?"

"Benjamin?" I can hear the complaint in my voice, but it's too late to nip it.

"Yes. One more person at the table won't hurt anything."

"So maybe I should invite someone too?" I suggest this knowing I must be sounding pretty cheeky—and I'm get-ting really aggravated at myself since I wanted to stop acting so self-centered. Unfortunately, changes like this don't always come easily. At least not for me.

"Sure, you can invite someone if you want. I've made enough pasta to feed an army."

So, without giving this much thought, I call Blake, and the next thing I know he's on his way to our house for dinner, and I am setting the dining room table with six places.

"This will be nice," Mom says happily. "Three guys and three girls."

"Need some help?" offers Paige when she finally emerges from her room. Naturally, she looks like she's ready to audition for *America's Next Top Model*. Yet, instead of offering a snarky comment, I tell her she looks pretty.

"Thanks! Why don't I take over for you," she offers. "That way you can go fix up some."

"Meaning I *need* to?" I tease.

She pats my cheek like I'm about six years old. "No, you look just fine for a little earth muffin."

I hand her the water pitcher. "Thanks. I can take a hint."

She just laughs as I go to my room to figure out whether I really want to be a "little earth muffin" tonight or not. Finally, I decide that a little spiffing up probably wouldn't hurt my image.

It's around eight by the time all six of us are at the table, and everyone seems to be getting along nicely. And I can tell this makes Mom happy. Jon seems like a genuinely nice guy. He seems interested in *Malibu Beach* as well as *On the Runway*, and he even includes Blake in the conversations too, asking him about where he thinks TV is headed. I can tell Blake appreciates this. I also like the way Jon is treating my mom. He's respectful and thoughtful and in some ways he's a lot like Dad. I guess that shouldn't surprise me. After all, why would Mom settle for anything less?

All in all, it's a pleasant meal and it's even fun watching *Malibu Beach* together afterward — and it turns out that both Paige and I end up in some of the scenes. Including the part where I stood up for my sister, which isn't easy to watch. Partly because it was an uncomfortable moment, and partly because I don't enjoy seeing myself on the screen. But that's not the situation with Paige. She's thrilled to see herself. And it's obvious the camera loves Paige. In fact, I think the camera loves Paige even more than Mia.

In the end, I have to admit that I like Benjamin more than I expected. He's polite and considerate and if it weren't for the Mia factor, I'd welcome him with open arms. Not that he's asking me to. I can kind of see why Paige is attracted to him, and I have to admit they make a stunning couple — in that Hollywood sort of way.

We've just turned off the TV and are back at the table having dessert when someone's cell phone rings, one of Mom's pet peeves on a night when she's fixed a real dinner. But it turns out to be my phone, and to my surprise it's Mollie.

"What's up?" she asks cheerfully.

"Hey! Great to hear from you. We're having dessert right now, so can I call you back?" I say this quietly, knowing that Mom's eying me and wondering why my phone wasn't turned off.

"Sure." Her voice sounds stiff.

"Okay. Soon as we're done." Then I hang up, turn off my phone, and go back to the table. "Sorry, Mom," I say, "I forgot it was on."

"Jon was just saying that he should schedule you and Paige to be on the morning show," Mom tells me as I sit down.

"Oh?"

"For publicity," she continues.

"Yes," Jon adjusts his dark-rimmed glasses. "I thought we could do a spot on you girls right before the Golden Globes. That might be fun."

"That sounds fabulous," Paige gushes. "I can hardly believe that we're going to be at the Golden Globes."

"Just on the red carpet," I remind her. "It's not like we get to go inside like the real guests."

"Not this year." She smiles slyly. "But just you wait ... one of these years."

Jon laughs. "I wouldn't doubt it after seeing you on *Malibu Beach* tonight."

"We've been invited to the Golden Globes too," Benjamin injects.

"The whole *Malibu Beach* show?" Jon asks in surprise.

"No ... just Mia and me."

Paige sits a little straighter, almost as if this is news to her.

"Won't that be a little awkward?" I ask, knowing I should probably just keep my mouth shut. But, hey, I'm curious. "I mean, if you guys have broken up?"

"The breakup will happen after the Golden Globes," Benjamin says this as if he's describing an episode and not a personal relationship, and I'm thinking maybe Mom was right about Mia acting after all. "Our director thought that would be better."

I want to ask him if Mia agreed with this, but I know that would be stepping over the line. Besides, I'm trying to be kinder and less judgmental—and it's none of my business anyway.

We continue the discussion, talking about who's been nominated for what and who everyone thinks will win and why. It's after ten by the time we finally start saying good-night, only because Jon informs us he has to get up in six hours to be ready for the morning show. But as he tells Mom good-night, I'm surprised to see them exchange a kiss. A real kiss. And it's kind of surreal. I mean, I've never seen my mom kiss anyone except for my dad. I suppose it's kind of upsetting too, but I try to act natural as I offer to walk Blake downstairs. Mostly I want to get away and just let this strangeness of this settle.

"Is it weird seeing your mom dating?" Blake asks as we stand in the courtyard by the parking lot.

I nod. "Yeah. I guess I wasn't as ready for it as I thought."

"Jon seems like a great guy."

"Yeah . . ." I look over at the stand of palm trees being lit by the spotlight. And then I notice that Benjamin and Paige are coming down the stairs. I assume, like me, she came down to give Mom some space and to tell Benjamin good-night in private. But the next thing I know she hops into his Porsche and off they go.

"Wonder what they're up to?" Blake asks.

"No idea," I say, trying to relax some of my overly protective-sister attitude.

Now Blake takes my hand and I'm not sure what he's about to do, but to my relief he just shakes it with both hands. "Thanks for a great evening, Erin. It was fun seeing you and Paige in your big debut."

"Thank you for coming," I say as he releases my hand.

We just stand there for a couple of minutes and I'm actually wondering if I want to move this up a notch—maybe I really do want him to kiss me like he used to do back before he broke my heart. On second thought, maybe I'm not ready for that yet. Just then Jon comes down the stairs. He calls out "good-night," then gets into his car and leaves.

"I should go back in," I say lamely.

"I'll watch until you go up the stairs," Blake offers.

"Oh, it's perfectly safe here," I assure him.

But he just smiles. "Maybe I just want to watch."

I laugh. "Okay then." I call out good-night as I hurry up

the stairs. And I'm still thinking about the boyfriend thing. Maybe I've been wrong about this. Maybe it is time to elevate Blake back up to "boyfriend" status. Or maybe not.

"So ..." Mom is cleaning up the dinner things. "What did you think of Jon?"

"He's great," I tell her as I start to load the dishwasher.

"Does it bother you though?" She continues rinsing something in the sink. "I mean because he's not your dad?"

"I guess it kind of took me by surprise," I admit, trying to be mature about the whole thing. "But that's probably natural."

She just nods.

"Hey, listen," I say. "You have to get up early tomorrow. Why don't I finish up in here?"

She turns to me with what seem like misty eyes. "Thanks, Erin." And then she hugs me. "I appreciate it."

As I work in the kitchen I wonder why my mom got misty over me offering to do the dishes, and I also wonder about my sister and Benjamin. If they were a normal couple, I might assume they went to a club. But because they're still staying beneath the radar, I doubt this. Unless they both simultaneously lost their minds—and that's possible. Finally, instead of obsessing and getting mad, I decide to just pray for them. Then I finish up the kitchen and go to bed.

The next morning I wake up to the sound of our doorbell ringing. I look at the clock to see that it's nearly ten. So, knowing Mom is long gone and Paige is probably sleeping in since I heard her roll in around one, I get up to see who's disturbing my sleep.

"Mollie?" I say in surprise. "Hi! Don't you have classes today?"

"Not until one." Without waiting for an invitation, she comes inside as if she's on a mission.

"Want some coffee?" I offer as I head for the kitchen.

"Why didn't you call me back last night?" she demands as she tosses her jacket onto the back of a counter stool and sits down.

"Oh, yeah!" I slap my forehead. "I totally forgot. Last night was kind of crazy." So as I fill the coffee carafe, I explain about who was here for dinner and how Paige is dating Benjamin and Mom's dating Jon and that I've been talking to Blake again. "And it was late and I went to bed." I click on the coffee maker, turn around, and hold up my hands and just smile. "Sorry about that."

"So Benjamin was *here* last night?" Her brow is creased like this is a big concern. And it's not that I don't agree, but I wonder why she should care so much.

I nod. "Yeah."

"But after that, he and Paige went out, right?"

"How do you know—"

"*Everyone* knows."

"Huh?"

"You mean *you* don't know?"

"Know what?"

"About your sister and Benjamin Kross."

"Of course I know. But how do *you* know?"

"Because someone tweeted me and then I went online. One of the gossip sites has a photo of the two of them sneaking into an all-night diner. I'm sure it's already all over the place."

"Seriously?" I lean forward on the breakfast bar and just stare at her. She seems to be enjoying being the bearer of bad news.

"Go get your laptop," she says eagerly. "I'll show you."

Then, as we're sitting there sipping coffee and perusing the gossip sites where news of Benjamin Kross's new romance is spreading like wildfire, Paige comes meandering out of her bedroom, looking just as lovely as ever even though I know she just crawled out of bed.

"Morning girls," she says sleepily.

"Paige," I say. "Uh, you better come look at this."

"What?" She yawns as she comes over to join us, leaning over to see the screen better. Then suddenly she stands erect. "Oh no ..."

"Oh yes." I nod at her trying to withhold an I-told-you-so expression.

Paige lets a swear word escape. "Sorry," she says quickly. "But this is *so* not good."

"Ya think?" I go back for another cup of coffee.

Paige sits down on a stool next to Mollie and stares blankly at the granite countertop.

"So what do you think?" Mollie says lightly. "*Are* you the next Angelina Jolie?"

"That was so last decade," I say. "Couldn't they come up with a more recent couple-crasher?"

"I'm *not* a couple-crasher," Paige says quietly.

"Well, Benjamin and Mia are still seen as a couple in the public's eyes," I remind her.

"And in Mia's eyes, it says here," Mollie points to the screen. "Want me to read it?"

Paige doesn't answer, but I nod. We might as well get this over with.

"Mia is quoted as saying that *Paige Forrester is a manipulative, backstabbing little witch.* And then she goes on to say that you're a frenemy and that you crashed her birthday party, pretended to be her friend, and went behind her back to steal her boyfriend." Mollie just shakes her head now. "And she also says that she hopes your show is cancelled or that they can at least find a host who knows how to behave herself better in both public and private and yada-yada."

"This is such a mess." Paige says.

I take a sip of coffee and wonder how my smooth sister is going to slip out of this mess.

Paige's phone is ringing, but she just sits there.

Before long, our landline rings and I pick it up with an approving nod from Paige. "I have Helen Hudson for Paige Forrester," Sabrina says stiffly.

"Just a minute," I say as I hold the phone toward my sister and mouth "Helen."

But she just stands up, shakes her head, then runs back to her room.

"I'm sorry," I say into the phone. "She's unable to — "

"Listen, Erin," Sabrina snarls, "tell Paige to get her little — "

"I'll have her call you back, okay?"

"Get her on the phone *now*," she seethes.

"I'll try. Hold on." I go and knock on Paige's door. "You have to take this call," I tell Paige. Then I open the door, finding my sister in a heap on her bed. "It's Helen Hudson," I say firmly. "And you need to talk to her."

Paige sits up and reluctantly holds her hand out for the phone, but her expression is like I'm handing her a loaded gun that she's about to place against her head.

"Just get it over with," I say gently. "Really, how bad can it be?" I place the phone in her hands, then force a little smile. "And I'll be praying for you, okay?"

She nods blankly and mutters into the phone, "This is Paige."

I consider sticking around to eavesdrop, but then decide Paige probably doesn't need any additional pressure right now. Besides, I said I'd pray for her. So I go back out and tell Mollie about my promise and the two of us bow our heads and ask God to help Paige through this difficult situation that she seems to have gotten herself into.

Chapter 16

"Helen wants to pull the plug on our show," Paige tells me after about an hour-long conversation. "Rather, she wants to pull the plug on me."

"Oh." I'm telling myself not to get mad. This is not as much about me right now as it is about Paige. After all, this was her dream, not mine. I was just coming along for the ride—the rollercoaster ride. Right now, I'm here to support her . . . no matter how culpable she is.

"I don't know what to do, Erin." Paige looks at me with a tear-streaked face and puffy eyes. No longer quite as picture-perfect as usual. Not that this makes me happy—I may have my little streaks of jealousy, but I would much rather see my sister happy and beautiful than miserable and looking like this.

"I wish I could stick around and see how this ends," Mollie says as she reaches for her jacket, "but I have to get to class. Good luck, Paige," she says softly.

"Thanks." Paige shakes her head.

"So Helen was really mad?"

"Oh ... yeah. The producer of *Malibu Beach* called her and accused her of trying to undermine their show in order to promote ours."

"That is so ridiculous."

"I told her that. But she said that in the cutthroat world of reality TV, anything is possible."

"Meaning she thinks you did this on purpose?"

"I told her that we were trying to keep our relationship under wraps."

"But, Paige, this is Hollywood, there is no such thing. And you know how connected Mia is. It probably took her five minutes to figure it out."

"I know ... and I feel stupid enough. You don't have to rub it in."

"Sorry, I just thought you knew what you were doing." I study my downcast sister and wonder if there was possibly something Freudian about this. Maybe she really didn't want to have her own show. Maybe this was just a handy escape route. And yet ... that just doesn't seem like her to me. No, I think it was just a dumb mistake.

"At least you weren't at a club," I point out, "drinking and dancing and acting like Lindsay Lohan."

"Helen actually said that exact thing."

"That's something."

"Unfortunately, it's not enough." Paige looks at me with fresh tears filling her eyes. "I wanted this show so bad, Erin. I can't believe I blew it like this. I really do like Benjamin. And it seemed perfectly safe. We were being so careful and only going to places where paparazzi have never been seen before. And honestly, I never saw anyone with a camera."

"But, Paige," I tell her, "*think* about it. All it takes is one person to snap a quick photo on a phone and it's all over. You don't need paparazzi."

"That's true. And if there were do-overs, I'd go back and do this whole thing differently. I would tell Benjamin that we had to wait."

"That's reassuring ... not that it helps much now." The landline phone rings again. I check to see that it's Mom and figure she must've heard the news. "Hi, Mom," I say in a flat voice.

"Oh, dear," she says quickly, "how is Paige?"

"Falling apart."

"Have you heard from the studio?"

"Sounds like Helen's pulling the plug on the show." I glance at Paige, but she's staring at the countertop again. "Or maybe she's just pulling the plug on Paige and me."

"This is too bad. I guess you were right after all, Erin."

"I wish I'd been wrong."

"Well, there's not much we can do about this. But I'm glad you're there with your sister. Give her a hug for me."

"Okay." Then we say good-bye and hang up.

"What am I going to do?" Paige says. I can't tell if she's talking to me or herself, but she says it over and over ... and I have no response.

Eventually, I go to my room. Although I feel sorry for Paige, I also can't get past the fact that she brought this on herself, and she brought it onto me too. Finally, I realize the only positive action I can take at the moment is to pray. I text Blake, who is probably in class now, asking him to pray too.

It's hard to know how to pray. I mean, I honestly feel like my sister made a wrong and selfish choice and the pain and suffering she's experiencing as a result only seems fair. Of course,

I wouldn't say that to her. That'd be kind of like kicking someone who'd fallen down. But as I try to pray, I'm confused. I'm
so frustrated that I actually get down on my knees—and I
don't usually do that to pray. I ask God to help me to pray and
to help me not to judge my sister, and then I remember a Bible
verse about how God can take something bad and turn it into
something good. So I ask him to use this mess to get Paige's
attention and to hopefully teach her something.

"What are you doing?"

I look up from where I'm still kneeling by the bed. "Huh?"

"What are you doing?" Paige asks again.

"Praying." I bow my head and silently say, "amen," and
then stand.

"Do you think it really works?"

"Prayer?" I'm thinking this could turn into a good conversation if I don't blow it by getting all defensive. I silently ask
God to help me.

"Yeah. Does God really listen or is it just to make you feel
better?"

"I think maybe both. But, yes, I do think God listens."

"Huh. I mean, I do believe in God. But I haven't prayed
since I was a little kid. Honestly, I don't see how praying can
change anything."

"Maybe you should give it another try."

"What were you praying for?"

I consider my answer. "Well ... mostly for you. I was asking God to bring something good out of this whole mess."

She sits on my bed. "Like that's even possible."

"All things are possible with God."

She just sits there staring at her hands lying limply in
her lap.

I wish I could think of something encouraging or positive to say to her, but I am completely blank now.

"I wish I could believe that, Erin."

"What?"

"What you just said … all things are possible with God. I wish I had that kind of faith … like you do."

"Then you should ask God to give it to you. If you ask God for faith, he'll give it to you."

"Just like that? He'll just give it to me?"

I'm trying to remember how the Bible verse goes that describes this. "The Bible explains it like this," I begin slowly. "It's like if you were a kid and you were hungry and you asked your parents for food, they wouldn't give you a rock to eat. Right?"

"Right."

"It's like that with God too. If you ask him for faith, he's not going to give you like, say, a toothache instead. At least I don't think so. But I also think you have to mean it when you ask. You probably can't just flippantly ask him, like you're testing to see if he'll really do it. I think you need to be sincere."

She nods real slowly, like she's trying to wrap her head around this. I'm feeling hopeful, like maybe God really is at work here, bringing something good out of something bad. Because, honestly, I can't remember a time when Paige really listened to me talk about God.

"I am sorry for what I did … for getting involved with Benjamin … for hurting Mia like that. I know it was wrong now, and I remember how you tried to warn me … but …"

I press my lips together and wait for her to continue.

"I wish I'd listened to you, Erin. I wish I'd done it differently."

"I guess this might be one of those school of hard knocks lessons, huh?"

"I guess ..."

Just then the phone rings, the landline again. "Should I answer it?" I ask Paige, but she shrugs. I go and get it.

"Erin, this is Helen Hudson."

"Do you want Paige?"

"No, I'd rather to talk to you first. You're the girl who seems to have her head on her shoulders."

"Uh, okay."

"We might be getting a second chance with *Malibu Beach*."

"A second chance?"

"To straighten things up. Well, actually it's more about messing things up, but I don't need to go into all that right now. But here's what we're thinking. If you and Paige could go over to where they're filming this afternoon and if Paige and Mia could, well, talk things over with the cameras running, perhaps we can work this out in a way that makes everyone happy."

"Is Mia even willing to do that?"

"Apparently, she is."

I have images of Mia and her friends jumping my sister and beating the living daylights out of her. Okay, I might be too imaginative, but I saw that on YouTube once and it was seriously messed up. "What if Mia wants to hurt Paige?"

"I'm sure Mia *does* want to hurt Paige. And Paige has certainly hurt Mia, don't you think?"

"Yes. But I mean physically. What if Mia and her friends beat Paige up while the cameras roll?"

"Oh, I seriously doubt that Rod would allow that."

"He might if he thought the fans would love it."

She chuckles. "I'm sure the fans *would* love it."

"So, how can you be sure it wouldn't happen?"

"I'm relatively certain, Erin." She gives me an exasperated sigh like this should all be very obvious. "And yes, I'm sure they will make her uncomfortable. But in all fairness, Paige should have to suffer a bit, don't you think?"

"She's already suffering."

"Privately maybe. But not in the public eye. She might need to do a little suffering that everyone can see."

"Yes … I can understand that." I'm starting to feel like I'm Paige's advocate now, negotiating a deal or a settlement or something. Like, okay, we'll agree to one fistful of hair in exchange for publicity immunity. "But I just want to know that no one will get physically hurt. Is there a way you can guarantee that?"

"I suppose that could be arranged."

"In that case, I think I can talk Paige into doing this. But I have one condition."

"Have you ever considered becoming an agent, Erin?" She chuckles again. "I think you'd be good at it."

"Maybe we need an agent," I tell her.

"Or an attorney if Paige doesn't watch out. So, tell me, what one condition?"

"I want my mom there when they're filming."

"You are a smart little cookie, aren't you?"

"I try."

"Fine then. Let me call the powers that be and see what we can agree to. In the meantime, you go tell that sister of yours what's up, okay?"

"Okay."

"And I have to say, Erin, that if we proceed with *On the Runway*—and that's still a big if—but if we continue as planned with Paige Forrester at the helm, I want you *by her side*, do you understand?"

"Meaning I'm supposed to keep her out of trouble? Because seriously, I'm not sure that's possible."

"Yes . . . yes . . . I know you're not her conscience, Erin, but if I start calling you Jiminy Cricket, don't be too surprised."

"Right."

"Good-bye, Jiminy." And she hangs up.

I return to my bedroom to find Paige still sitting on my bed with a dazed expression. So I tell her about this latest invitation.

"But Mia will probably want to kill me."

"I'm sure she will. And I told Helen that we need some assurance that you won't be physically assaulted like those videos on YouTube where a girl is accosted by a bunch of her so-called friends."

"Oh, wouldn't the *Malibu Beach* fans love that. Mia and Benjamin are like the dream couple, and I'm like the wicked witch who broke them up. I'm sure the fans would love to see me beat beyond recognition."

"Just the seriously disturbed ones. So anyway, Helen is going to talk to *Malibu's* director and get back to us. Also, I told Helen that if we do this, Mom has to be on the set too."

"Great idea, Erin." Paige gives me a wimpy high five. "So, if we do this, does that mean we get our show back?"

"Helen's not making any promises. I suspect it will have to do with how this thing at *Malibu Beach* plays out."

"Right . . ." Paige stands and she begins pacing as if she's thinking really hard, as if she's plotting some clever way to turn this whole thing in her favor and come out on top. Although I'm pretty sure that's impossible.

It's after two when Helen calls back. The news is that *Malibu Beach* wants us at their location, Mia's house, at four o'clock sharp. I write down the address as she continues. "Filming begins as soon as Paige and you walk into the house. Your mother will arrive earlier so that they can tuck her out of sight of the cameras. And she is not to intervene unless there is actual threat of physical violence, which Rod assures me will not happen."

"Okay. I'll have to call my mom and make sure she can do this."

"I already took that liberty. She will be there."

"Good." And it's not that I don't trust Helen, but I also make note to double-check that Mom is actually in the loop.

"There won't be time for you to come to the studio for wardrobe, but I'm sure Paige can figure something out. Remember this scene is almost absolutely certain to air. What happens today will either make or break Paige Forrester. But she is on her own. Understand?"

"On her own, except that I'm with her, you mean?"

"Yes. You're both on your own. Make me proud … or walk. You got that?"

"Yes, ma'am."

"I'm not holding my breath. Good-bye, Jiminy." And, again, she hangs up before I can even say good-bye. I'm not holding my breath either. In fact, I take in a deep one as I mentally prepare myself for four o'clock.

Paige throws us into high gear, picking outfits, doing hair, makeup, and the whole time it's hard to believe this is the same girl who fell apart earlier. As she's helping with my makeup I ask if she's heard from Benjamin since this all hit the fan.

"No ..." she says slowly as she applies eyeliner, something I never can seem to get quite right.

"Nothing at all?" I want to ask her whether or not she thinks that's odd, considering that Benjamin is also a vital part of this whole cheaters scandal. I mean, it does take two.

"Well he texted me ..."

"And?"

"And he's been advised not to speak to me ... for the sake of his show and his reputation."

"Oh." I vaguely wonder if this might not actually be some kind of cleverly crafted setup. Like maybe they were just using Paige as part of the love triangle to get some great publicity. But I don't want to derail Paige, or shake her confidence, by mentioning it.

I offer to drive us to Mia's house, but I borrow Mom's portable GPS for direction assistance since we have to walk in that door at four on the dot. Paige is extremely quiet as I drive. I want to suggest that she pray, but I'm not sure how she'd receive that right now. So as the electronic lady tells me to turn here or exit there, I ask God to bring good out of bad and to use this to bring Paige to a place where she asks God for faith as well as help. Because, just like the rest of us, the girl needs some.

"Ready for this?" she asks me as she rings the doorbell.

"I hope so." I glance nervously at her. She, as usual, is gorgeous. Suddenly we are walking into Mia's house, and what I'm hoping isn't really a trap. But it is reassuring to know Mom's there. She told me she had to take time off work, but felt it was worth it.

With lights on and cameras rolling, I brace myself for the big showdown. Let the fireworks begin!

Chapter 17

"*What are you doing here?*" *Mia demands* as soon as Paige and I go into the great room where it seems the fun is about to begin. I know Mia is in the know and fully aware that we're supposed to be here. I assume her dramatic statement is just for the cameras.

"I want to talk," Paige says calmly.

"Oh, I'll just bet you do." Mia narrows her eyes. "But if you think you can talk your way out of this, you're crazier than I thought you were." Mia then softens. "And I thought you were my friend, Paige."

"I want to be your friend," Paige says.

"More like *frenemy.*"

"I'm sorry about all—"

"I don't want to hear it," Mia says quickly. "I'm not ready to hear an apology from you."

"What do you want then?" Paige holds her hands out.

"I want to know why you did this to me. Why did you act like you wanted to be friends? The whole time you were plotting to steal Benjamin."

"I wasn't plotting anything, Mia. I can't help it that Ben and I hit if off."

"Yeah, right." Mia shakes her head. "I trusted you, Paige. You came to my birthday party and you told me sweet things and I totally believed you. And then you stabbed me in the back." Mia actually looks like she's about to cry. Brogan and Natasha, who've been standing nearby, move in closer, as if this has all been prearranged . . . staged.

"Benjamin and I have been together for, like, forever. It's been more than two years. How many people our age can claim something like that? Our families are friends and everyone knows that we'll probably get married someday."

"I'm sorry," Paige says again. "I know this has hurt you, Mia. But Ben and I fell in love. It's not like we planned it. It just happened."

"Fell in love?" Mia looks at her friends like this is shocking, and I am equally as shocked. *In love?* "You think that Benjamin's in love with you?"

Paige shrugs. "That's what he told me."

Mia's brows arch and her blue eyes get bigger. "Right. He's in love with you. Do you know how totally ridiculous that makes you sound? That you actually *believe* Benjamin Kross is in love with you?"

Paige is caught off guard now. I can see it in her eyes. "That's what he told me, Mia. That he loved me . . . and that he no longer loved you . . . that it was over between you two. I'm sorry if that hurts. I honestly never wanted to hurt you, but it's the truth."

Mia actually laughs. So much for the teary act. "I cannot believe you fell for that, Paige. I actually thought you were smarter."

"Fell for what?"

"For Benjamin's line about loving you ... and not loving me. Who would have thought you'd be suckered in. But they say a new sucker is born every day, right?"

Paige shrugs again and glances over her shoulder to me, like maybe I can help. But I don't see how. More than ever, I wish I had a camera to hold in front of me. Then I remember what Helen said, how I'm supposed to stand by Paige's side. And so I step up. "Let me get this clear," I say to Mia. "You're suggesting this thing between my sister and Benjamin was just an act, like he really wasn't into her, like he was pretending?"

"Oh, I get it. One sister got the brains and the other one got the beauty ... or so she thinks," Mia says to her friends and, of course, they laugh.

"So, let me guess," I continue. "If what you're saying is true, which I doubt, Benjamin led Paige on so that your show could get more publicity? This is all just a stunt to raise ratings?"

Mia acts surprised. "Of course not. I'm saying that Benjamin was simply using Paige. That's all. Old story. Happens all the time." Mia turns to Paige now. "So, you see, you're the one who's been hurt here. Not me. Well, other than the fact that you've turned out to be a backstabbing little boyfriend-stealer. And that you were only pretending to be my friend, but were really just using me. I'm guessing you were using Benjamin too. I'm sure you hoped that hooking up with a star would make you a star. Unfortunately, you were wrong."

"I really don't understand what you're saying." Paige says this in a way that's so genuine, I almost feel like crying. "But I am sorry if I hurt you. I don't expect you to believe me. Benjamin told me that it was only a matter of time until he

172

broke it off with you, that he had to keep up the appearance of a romance for the sake of your show and that he would eventually break up officially. But I realize now that it was still wrong for me to get involved with him. I should've waited. We should've waited."

"You really are delusional, aren't you?" Mia turns to her friends. "Can you guys believe this?"

"Maybe someone dropped her on her head as a baby," suggests Natasha.

"Or maybe she's just trying to milk this for all she can," says Brogan.

"Or maybe she doesn't believe you," I say to Mia. "I mean, you're talking for Benjamin, aren't you? Why isn't he here to talk for himself?" I glance around the room. "What did you do anyway? Did you tie him up and gag him and toss him into the cellar?"

"Very funny." Mia looks at me like I'm something disgusting stuck to the bottom of her shoe.

"Then why should we believe what you're saying about Benjamin?" I persist. "Why can't he speak for himself?"

"Yes," Paige agrees. "Why can't he? Not that I want to see you hurt anymore, Mia. I really don't. And whether or not you forgive me, I am honestly sorry for all this. And I plan to tell Ben that he and I cannot date until he officially breaks things off with you."

Mia laughs loudly, and so do her friends. "You really are naïve, aren't you, Paige? You're still buying into the fantasy that Benjamin seriously liked you. Oh, wait, make that 'loved' you. You thought he loved you!" She shakes her head with a look of disbelief. "Really, this is classic!"

"Then why don't we get Benjamin to come over here."

I'm reaching for my cell phone, like I'm going to call him, which is totally bogus since I don't even have his number. "And, once and for all, we can set things straight."

"Good idea, Erin. You are such a smart little Nerd Girl. Yes, let's get Benjamin in here to set things straight, shall we?" She nods toward a darkened hallway. "Hey there, honey," she calls out. "Have you heard enough yet? Come out, come out, wherever you are."

And that's when I know. This really is a setup. A sting. And they are about to get Paige — and get her good.

Benjamin strides out now and, going directly to Mia, puts an arm around her, then leans down and kisses her on the lips. I'm no expert, but it looks like he means it. I glance over at Paige and I can honestly see her face getting pale beneath her tan and makeup.

"How does it feel?" Natasha asks Paige.

"Yes." Brogan's eyes narrow. "How *does* it feel?"

"Benjamin?" Paige's voice comes out in a whisper. "Is it true? Is everything Mia just said really true?"

He makes a sheepish little smile then nods. "Sorry about that."

Then Paige turns and runs out and I hear the front door slam. And for a split second, I'm torn. I want to run after her and tell her to forget this whole thing. And yet, my work here isn't done.

I step up to Benjamin, looking him straight in the eyes. "You are a lying two-faced hypocrite," I calmly tell him. "And a first-class jerk. You chased after Paige and you know it. You called her. You took her out. And you even came to dinner at our house, and I can prove it. I saw you kiss her and I heard you say sweet things to her and I have to admit that I fell for your act too. I thought you were a nice guy and I actually believed that you meant what you said to her. I guess that proves you really are a talented actor, but as a human being, you are a total wipeout … a loser and a user and a lowlife and—and I wish my sister had never met you."

Mia laughs at this. "Wow, you're a long-winded little thing, aren't you, Nerd Girl?"

I turn to her now. "And I'm sure that everything I say today will never make it on the air," I say calmly. "Actually, I'm glad for that. But, as for you, what my sister said to you was true. She truly was sorry. And she's not a mean person. She did not plot against you. Yes, she made a mistake, but she was honestly sorry for it. And when she came to your birthday party, she was sincere. She really did want to be your friend. She, unlike *some people*, was not faking it."

Benjamin is about to say something, but I cut him off, swinging my finger under his nose. At this point, I don't care how *nerdy* I seem. "And you know what I think? I think you and Mia deserve each other. Yes, you are a perfect match. Selfish, ruthless, conniving, publicity-seeking opportunists who will use anyone just so you can get one more photo of yourselves. You will stoop to anything just to increase your ratings and fan base. How you can look at yourself in the mirror or even sleep at night is a mystery to me. And I feel sorry for you when you finally figure out that this is all fleeting and unreal. And you will eventually. Eventually, you *will* be sorry. Because when you sell your soul to the Devil, you eventually have to pay up."

Then I turn and am ready to storm out after Paige, but Benjamin calls out, "Erin, stop." And something in his voice makes me stop and turn around.

His arm isn't around Mia now, and he takes a step toward me. "I'm sorry, Erin," he says quietly.

"Benjamin!" Mia's voice is strained.

"You're right," he continues. "I am all those things you just said—and more."

"Benjamin," she says again, louder now as if he's suddenly lost his hearing. "We discussed this already. *Remember?*"

He glances back at her. "I'm sorry, Mia. But I can't do this anymore. Erin nailed it. I do feel like I sold out. Like I'm selling my soul to the Devil for a little bit of fame. And I refuse to keep doing it. It's wrong."

I feel like someone just pulled the floor out from under me. Is this for real? Or am I getting scammed just like Paige did? "Whatever," I say. I don't trust him yet.

"For real. I am sorry," he says in a contrite voice. But then, I remind myself, he is an actor. And reality TV, well, it's not always as real as it seems.

"I did tell Paige that I loved her," he continues. "And I told her that I wanted to break up with Mia. Mia knew all that. But what she doesn't know is .. I did fall for Paige. "

"You did not!" Mia steps closer to him. "Liar!"

"Everything Paige said was true. I fell for her—the moment I met her I was swept away. She's sweet and genuine and fun. Mia, I haven't been in love with you for ..." he pauses to think. "Well, months anyway. I just played it that way because we know that's what fans want. Always give them what they want, right?"

"But you told me that the whole thing with Paige was just a publicity stunt!" Mia is fuming. *"You lied to me."*

"I had to. You wouldn't accept anything else." He shakes his head. "And I'm not proud of it. I can't imagine how hurt Paige feels. She'll probably never forgive me."

I feel lightheaded. *Is this really happening?* I glance over to see cameras are still running. And their director Rod looks pleased, like this is even better than he expected.

"I hate you!" Mia screams at Benjamin. And then she begins swinging her fists and yelling some really foul words that may or may not end up on the cutting-room floor.

"I have to get Paige," I call to no one in particular. Maybe Mom, although I haven't spotted her yet.

"Tell her I'm sorry," Benjamin yells back. Then, as I reach for the door, he lets out a yelp that sounds like Mia just landed a solid slap. I sort of wish I could've seen it, but right now I just need to find my sister.

Chapter 18

"I've looked everywhere for her," I tell Mom. It's nearly seven and dark out, and Paige is still missing. I drove all through Mia's neighborhood, expecting to find her wandering the streets and sobbing. I even went to look for her on the beach, but it was raining and the beach was deserted. Then hoping she'd taken a taxi home, I came back here. But it's obvious she hasn't been home.

"And her phone is still going straight to voicemail," Mom says in a worried voice. "The light just turned green so I should probably hang up before I cause an accident."

"Yes," I say urgently. The idea of having lost my dad, Paige missing, and my mom in a car wreck is more than I can handle. "Just come home, Mom. There's no way you're going to find her by driving all around."

"You're right. But I can't help but look as I drive. Although I can't imagine her out walking by herself in the rain. That just isn't Paige."

"But none of this is really Paige," I point out.

"Poor Paige. I wish she'd answer her phone."

"Hang up," I tell Mom. "Maybe she's trying to call you."

"Maybe. See you soon."

I start pacing in the kitchen. Like Mom, I'd rather go drive around looking for Paige, but I know that's ridiculous in a town this size. I've already called Blake and several others, begging them to pray for Paige. Because, I wouldn't be surprised if my sister's on the edge — teetering — and I really hope that she falls on God.

I continue to pace. Pace and pray. And as I pray for Paige, I realize how much I love my sister. I know we're different as night and day, and I know I sometimes make fun of her or call her shallow. But more than ever, I realize that I need Paige. It's like we're connected ... like yin and yang, like shadows and light in a black-and-white photo, it takes both to give dimension. My life would be flat without her. And despite all the trouble that comes with my sister, I really do love her. I so don't want to lose her.

"Look what I found!" Mom exclaims. I turn to see my sister — at least I think it's her, but it's hard to tell since she looks like a drowned rat.

"Oh, Paige!" I run and hug her. "I'm so glad you're okay."

She hugs me back, tightly holding onto me as if she missed me too. Then finally, she steps back and I'm thinking I'm almost as wet as she is. "Mom told me what you did, Erin."

"Go get out of those wet things," Mom insists. "Take a hot shower and I'll fix us all some soup. Then you and Erin can talk."

Paige doesn't argue and I help Mom make grilled-cheese sandwiches and tomato soup. It's one of our favorite "comfort" meals and I'm thinking I could use it tonight.

"I found Paige just a few blocks from home. Can you believe she walked all the way here from Mia's house?"

"No way."

"Yes. She said she wanted to think."

"Wow, that was a lot of thinking. Wet thinking."

"I only told her about how you dressed down those horrible kids, Erin." Mom reaches over and pats me on the back. "By the way, I can't remember ever being prouder of one of my daughters. I would've stood up and cheered, except that I promised to remain quiet." She chuckles. "Also, I didn't want to spoil the scene because I'm hoping they'll use it on the show."

"Oh, I seriously doubt that—"

"Don't be so sure. I was chatting with the director after the bloodshed, which by the way, there was."

"What? Bloodshed?" I'm partly horrified and partly curious. "Who? How?"

"Shortly after you left, Mia slugged Benjamin right in the nose. It looked like it might be broken."

"No way!"

Mom nods. "Yes, it got ugly. But once Benjamin's nose was spurting blood, the director stepped in and called it a wrap."

"Will they put *that* on the show?"

"It sounds like the whole thing, from you and Paige showing up until the nose punching, will air. The director was actually quite pleased with himself." Mom shook her head. "You'd think he'd planned the whole thing."

"He didn't, did he?"

"I really don't think so. I kept watching him as the whole thing was going on, hoping that he'd stop it earlier when you girls were still there, but I watched his face and he looked as shocked as anyone as to how it turned out. Shocked and pleased." She sadly shakes her head. "Reality TV is a strange beast. In some ways it's like the news ... only far more brutal."

Finally, Paige emerges looking warmer but still unhappy. While we eat our soup and sandwiches, Mom and I take turns replaying the whole thing for her, even to the part where Benjamin publicly declared his love for her. But still she doesn't seem to react.

"Aren't you happy?" I ask as I finish the last of my sandwich.

She just shrugs. "It feels like too little, too late."

"I must admit I wanted to wring that boy's neck," Mom says.

"Me too." I said.

"You did better than wring his neck, Erin," Mom tells me. "You brought him to his senses. That line about selling his soul to the Devil—well, it was just perfect."

"You said that to him?" Paige looks at me with wonder.

"That and a lot more," Mom confirms.

But still, Paige doesn't seem too happy. And I guess I can't blame her. Benjamin might've come around, but just moments before he was Mia's puppet, sacrificing Paige for his own welfare. Not a trait a girl likes in a boyfriend.

I'm helping Mom clean up after dinner when my cell phone rings. "Go ahead and get that," Paige tells me as she takes the saucepan away from me. "I'll finish up in here. It's the least I can do."

I look my phone and see that it's Blake. "Sorry, I forgot to call you," I quickly tell him. "Paige is home and fine."

"Good to know, but I thought I'd let you know that the gossip sites have already picked up the latest story. And I have to say, that sister of yours is coming out on top. Paige is smelling like a rose."

"Seriously?" I run to my room and turn on my laptop,

hunting for the site that he's currently looking at. And he's right. The tables have turned and now Mia is looking like the wicked witch and Paige is the victim. Isn't life funny.

But even after I hang up and go show the site to Paige, she's not really happy about it. I wonder if she'll ever be happy again. I also wonder who leaked this story.

It's not long until our home phone rings with Fran Bishop on the other end, saying that we're still on for the fashion show tomorrow.

"You're kidding," I tell her. "We're still invited to Mia's fashion show? How is that possible?"

"It's not really Mia's show," Fran informs me. "So it's not really her decision. And when it comes to publicity ... well, you know how it goes."

"Right."

"So, I want you girls at the studio around ten. Then we'll all drive over together. The show's supposed to start at one, and our crew will be all set up."

Once again, Paige isn't really happy when I tell her what should clearly be good news. "That means we're still doing the show," I say plainly, like maybe she doesn't really get this.

"That's good." She looks back down at the *Elle* magazine she's been flipping through.

"Are you okay?" I ask.

She just shrugs.

"Still hurting over Benjamin?"

Now she nods. "I've never been treated like that before, Erin. Aside from losing Daddy—and that's a whole different kind of pain—I can't remember feeling this hurt."

"It'll probably take some time," I tell her. "Has Benjamin called?"

"My phone's off."

"And he's probably in pain too." I'm primarily thinking of his nose.

She sighs and looks back at her fashion rag.

Paige continues to remain somber the next day. She's unusually quiet as we drive to the studio. And even as Fran helps pick out our outfits, stressing that today matters more than anything since it will be our first official *On the Runway* show—our premiere—Paige is like ho-hum.

"Paige?" Fran finally demands. "What is wrong with you, girl? It's like you're not even in there. Are you sure you're up for this?"

Now Paige smiles and starts to chatter away, as if hoping to convince Fran that all is well and that she really can pull this off. While Fran might be buying this little act, I know that's all it is. But hopefully no one else will be able to tell.

We arrive at the hotel where the fashion show is being held, and as we go through the lobby, one of our camera guys, Alistair, meets us and immediately goes into filming. And, remembering my role here, I follow suit. It's a comfort to have my camera to keep me busy—and to hide behind.

Meanwhile, Fran hurries ahead to make sure that all is ready in the fashion show area. Somehow Paige manages to keep her bubbly, chatty self going, talking to the camera as if she's talking to her new best friend (the viewer) as she discusses today's fashion show and what designers are being featured and, once again, I can't help but admire her grit. I couldn't pull that off if I was suffering a broken heart.

We're almost to the elevators when we see a guy

approaching and I think it must be Benjamin, although it's hard to tell because his face is so swollen and his nose is bandaged and his eyes are blackened. He literally looks like he was hit by a truck. A truck named Mia.

"Benjamin!" Paige gasps to see him. Then she subtly signals at Alistair to stop shooting. But he just keeps going like he thinks he's getting something good.

I put down my camera and actually place my hand over his lens. Knowing how much camera guys hate this, I know I'm taking a serious risk.

"Let's give them some privacy, please," I tell him. "It's not like we're the paparazzi, right?" Paige and Benjamin hurry off to a secluded area over by the bathrooms where, thankfully, no one seems to notice them. I thank Alistair for cooperating, then open my backpack, extract my camcorder, and begin asking him for some filming tips. This keeps us both busy for a few minutes and eventually Paige comes back, and to my relief, she looks a little happier. She's not yet her same old self, but something has changed. I'm hoping that means Benjamin gave her the full apology she deserved.

We go up the elevator and into the ballroom where the fashion show will be and where a number of people are already milling about, including some designers and other guests. Everything seems pretty much set with lights and sound technicians and cameras running and, like a pro, Paige immediately takes control of the situation. She begins talking to various Big Name people, discussing the latest fashion trends with them and even fielding, with wit, their own questions about her new show and personal life. We slowly make our way to the back and into a smaller room where the models are getting ready. It seems pretty hectic back here, but I just keep my camera focused on my sister and film her as she works this room just as efficiently as she did the other. And, in fact, all seems to be going smoothly. I feel like maybe I can breathe a little more easily.

That is until we see Mia and several of her friends, the "bighearted" ones who are "donating" their time as models this afternoon. So charitable of them. I'm wondering how Paige is going to handle this sticky situation. The simple solution would be to avoid them — and it would serve them right to lose their opportunity for extra publicity — but instead she heads straight for them. Not an easy feat considering they're clear in the back, where I'm sure they hoped to be overlooked by *On the Runway*.

"And here we have some of the stars of that immensely popular reality show, *Malibu Beach*," Paige says brightly. "In fact, Mia Renwick has generously helped to put today's fashion show together. Hello, Mia." Paige extends the handheld mic toward Mia. "You look absolutely beautiful today. That shade of blue is stunning. Can you tell us a little about what and who you're wearing, Mia?"

Mia looks stunned, but she quickly recovers and launches into a description of her silk-and-lace evening dress and the designer who made it. It's obviously not the one Paige gave her for her birthday; I'll bet that one might've gone up in smoke.

Paige moves on to the other girls, who've had a couple minutes to regain their composure, and they manage to answer the questions almost as flawlessly as Mia. And, amazingly, that's it. No name-calling, hair-pulling, swearing, or mean looks. Whether it's all just an act is anyone's guess, but these girls have on their best manners today. Go figure. Maybe their moms are in the next room.

The fashion show seems to come off just as smoothly as my sister's coverage of it. All in all, everyone seems pleased. It's also nice to know that the proceeds of the event are going to be donated to the Children's Miracle Network. Finally, Paige signs off by explaining that the next *On the Runway* event will be at the Golden Globes.

"And I hope to see you all there," she says happily. "In the meantime, keep putting your best foot forward." Our cameras move down to her long legs and zoom onto her shoes, just like Fran directed us earlier when we staged this final scene. Paige giggles as she points her toe and jiggles her foot for this shot. She's wearing a pair of pretty hot-pink pumps, although I don't get the bright red soles. Then our cameras zoom back to her face. "And in my case that would be *Christian Loubou-tin*." She makes a finger wave. "See you next time—*On the Runway*."

"Cut and that's a wrap!" Fran tells everyone. "That was great, Paige." She pats her on the back. "And, unless I'm mistaken, this premiere show is going to be a hit. I can't wait to hear Helen's reaction next week."

"Thanks." Paige is beaming. And I'm thinking she's mostly back. Okay, maybe not *totally* back. In a way, I think that's a good thing. I think maybe her old self actually decided to grow up just a bit. At least I hope so.

Chapter
19

$\mathscr{I}$ can't believe how quickly the On the Runway film editors went over what must've been hours and hours worth of film, magically reconstructing it into what turned out to be a cohesive and entertaining show. To my surprise, it looks as if some of my own camera footage actually made the cut. They also fit various excerpts from the *Malibu Beach* show into it, including some of the less-than-flattering Mia scenes. Finally, the show covered the fashion show, ending with the *put your best foot forward* line.

"Wonderful," Helen exclaims as the house lights come back on. We're in the studio's viewing room, which is actually like a mini theater, along with the rest of our crew.

"The editing was brilliant," Paige says. "Amazing."

"And that music was awesome," I add.

"Do you think we might actually have a hit on our hands?" Fran asks cautiously.

"We'll know the answer to that in a few days." Helen stands up. "Nice work, people. Now keep your fingers crossed."

As we walk down the hallway, Helen puts her arm around Paige's shoulders. "I have to say, I doubted that we'd get here." She chuckles. "It's certainly been a rollercoaster ride this last week—but you turned out to be a trooper. And if you keep it up . . . well, there's no telling where you'll end up."

"Thanks for not giving up on us, Helen." Paige smiles as she slips her arm around me, pulling me into their little love circle. "The truth is, I never would've made it without Erin."

"Oh, I'm fully aware of that." Helen winks at me. "Where would we be without our little Jiminy Cricket?"

"What?" Paige looks confused.

"Never mind," I tell her. Then we part ways and Paige and I head for the exit.

"I wish Mom could've been here," Paige says as we walk through the parking lot.

"She would've loved it. But she'll see it on Friday night."

"And then it's the Golden Globes on Sunday." Paige sighs as she unlocks her car. "Hopefully it will go as smoothly as the fashion show."

"Are you worried about Mia?" I ask hesitantly once we're in the car.

"Well, Benjamin said that their producer still expects them to go there together, but I can't even imagine how that will happen."

"Will you interview them on the red carpet?"

Paige kind of laughs. "Yeah, if I get the chance. Why not? I'm sure the viewers will get a kick out of it."

"Especially considering that the *Malibu Beach* breakup show airs tomorrow night."

"Can't wait to see that one." But her tone is sarcastic, and I can tell she's still not over the hurt. And, although Benjamin keeps calling and has even sent flowers, she's keeping him at a safe distance. Who could blame her?

On Thursday, it's just Mom, Paige, and me watching *Malibu Beach* together. I considered inviting Blake, but since Paige absolutely refused to invite Benjamin, and because I had no idea how the breakup show would turn out, it seemed wise to keep it private. As we sit and watch what turns out to be a very emotional show—so much so that all three of us end up in tears—I can see why their producer was so pleased.

"That was quite a show," I say as I turn the TV off. "I'm glad we recorded it—I think I might need to watch it again."

"Wow." Mom's blowing her nose. "I wouldn't be surprised if *Malibu Beach* tries to steal you girls from *On the Runway*."

"Like I'd do that." Paige shakes her head.

"One thing's for sure," Mom says, "we need to get you an agent ASAP. Jon has mentioned this a few times, but I think I'm beginning to see his point. I'll ask for some recommendations. Speaking of Jon, you girls should probably get your beauty sleep if you want to look good for your spot on his show tomorrow. Six a.m. will be here sooner than you expect."

On Friday morning, on our way back from doing the morning show, which seemed to go okay, Paige decides that it's okay for me to invite some friends over to watch the premiere of our first show tonight. Mom had suggested that I simply surprise Paige with a party, but since she is still dealing with the whole Benjamin-Mia thing, I didn't think that would be fair.

Paige rattles off some names of friends she'd like to invite, and we make a list that includes Lionel, Addison, and Mollie, and several others. Paige insists that Benjamin's name not to be on the guest list . . . not that I had planned on calling him. Mom does a quick scramble to gather up party food on her way home from work, and at 8:25 we cram about twenty people in front of our big-screen TV. But as the show is about to begin, I'm seriously worried. What if it's a flop and we just didn't realize it? What if everyone here hates it, but they're too embarrassed to say so? All this anxiety—or maybe it's the spicy meatballs we had for dinner—is making me feel sick.

I go to the back of the room and watch nervously as the ads come on. Helen is proud of our sponsors and I guess she should be, since without them there would be no show. I just hope they're not disappointed. I then realize that it's interesting that I should care this much, as not too long ago I didn't care whether the show made it or not. Now here I am shaking in my Uggs for fear that it will bomb. Go figure.

Our show does not bomb. Paige wows everyone in the room with her timing and wit and inexhaustible fashion knowledge. And I even get a few chuckles as Camera Girl when I trip over a lighting cord. Everyone here seems to genuinely like it, and when it ends, the room erupts in loud applause and cheers.

"That was great," Blake tells me as he joins me in the back of the room. "I think it's going to be a hit." He gives me a high five. "Congrats!"

"You weren't in it very much," Mollie mentions. "Not nearly how you were in *Malibu Beach*."

"And that's as it should be," I tell her. "It's Paige's show. I'm just the camera girl."

"Don't let her fool you," Paige calls out from where she's sitting with her friends and drinking in their praises. "I couldn't have done it without her. For those of you who watched that *Malibu Beach* episode yesterday, you know exactly what I'm talking about."

Suddenly that's what everyone is talking about, and I am so uncomfortable that I go out to the terrace just to escape. I do not like being the center of attention. I don't think I ever will. But as I watch my sister with our friends, I know that she thrives on it, and that's okay. I am glad to see her happy again. It feels like it's been more than a week since "the incident" with Benjamin and Mia. I wonder how long it will take her to fully recover, or how long it will take Benjamin to take a hint. Because, no matter how many roses and chocolates and cards he sends, I don't think Paige will ever get back together with him. At least I hope not.

Chapter

20

"I'm sorry," I tell Paige for about the tenth time. "I am not going to wear a gown to the Golden Globes. And don't keep begging me, okay?"

"Erin is right," Fran tells my sister as she holds out another pair of shoes for Paige to scrutinize. "It would look weird to see a photographer dressed formally. Erin needs to be able to move around and maneuver and get shots. She's not there to be in front of the camera, but behind it. But don't worry, I have a perfect outfit set out for her. Stylish yet casual."

Paige tosses a pout my way, then turns to check out her gown in the mirror. It's a pale green Armani Privé that shimmers and shines like a piece of jewelry. "That is really beautiful," I tell her, partly to distract her from her obsession of doing a sister act with me on the red carpet, and partly because it is really beautiful.

"Those Pradas will be perfect with the dress," Fran declares as Paige slips a foot into a pearly looking high-heeled sandal. With these decisions made and the gown and shoes safely set aside, Paige is moved on to makeup and hair.

"You too," Fran is now telling me.

"What?"

"Well, even though you're not wearing a gown, you can't go out there looking like that. Don't forget you are part of the show."

"That's right," Paige calls out from the makeup area, "and I don't want to put you on my fashion *faux pas* list."

"Like that would be something new."

Before long, we're dressed and ready and loaded into the limo with Fran. Paige is still studying her "cheat sheet": a list of celeb names and which designer they are reportedly wearing. It was Fran's idea, and at first Paige said she wouldn't need it, but she seems to have reconsidered.

"The camera crew is already there," Fran tells us. I wish I could've gone with them, but know better than to state this. Besides, strange as it seems, I think Paige needs me for this event too.

"This is so exciting," Paige says as Fran removes very expensive-looking earrings from a locked case. "I've never worn real diamonds before."

"Just make sure you don't lose them or you might never wear real ones again," Fran tells her.

Even though it's still too early for any real celebrities to show up on the red carpet, fans are lined up everywhere, and when Paige gets out of the limo, they call out to her, whistling and hooting and finally asking who she is.

She turns and smiles and waves. "I'm Paige Forrester for *On the Runway*."

"That's the girl who was on *Malibu Beach*," a female fan yells.

"And that's her sister," yells a guy. "The girl who told off Mia and Benjamin."

Several people clap and cheer. "Way to go!" a teen girl calls out.

"We're setting you girls up over here," Fran says, nudging us along to where our camera guys are already waiting. Then she gives us some brief direction, telling us where we can and cannot go. "I'll be over by the staging area, near where the celebs get out of the car, and I will attempt to direct the younger ones your way." She crosses her fingers. "Hopefully they'll have heard of our show by now and will be willing to cooperate. But don't be surprised if we don't get too many A-listers. Just make the most of whoever comes your way."

"Absolutely." Paige nods, taking this in. Although I doubt anyone else can tell, I know she's nervous. This is a big day for her.

"And you stay close to Paige," Fran reminds me. "I want you being shot as she's interviewing. I want to hear you two girls chatting to each other too. Keep that behind-the-scenes commentary going, Paige."

It seems like a long wait until the celebs begin to trickle in, but then it's like the dam breaks open and suddenly they are everywhere. Paige appears to remain calm and in control as she interviews the ones who come our way. Unfortunately, Fran was right; they are not the most-known names, but these stars seem to enjoy chatting with Paige, and I can tell she's feeling pretty comfortable.

"So, Miss Haley Bernard, what are you wearing tonight?" Paige asks a teenage girl who recently debuted in a movie that's up for an award.

The girl seems like a nervous wreck, like she's on totally foreign turf. "It's, uh, it's a retro gown by ..." She frowns. "I can't remember."

Paige smiles as she studies Haley's dress. "Let me guess . . . is it Chanel?"

"That's it!" Haley's posture relaxes a bit. "How did you know?"

"Fashion is my thing." Paige gives the actress a look of approval. "And I must say that you look fabulous, Haley. And good luck tonight—you're up against some stiff competition. But even if you don't win, you'll knock 'em dead with that dress."

"Really?" Haley still looks unsure.

"Trust me, you look totally hot."

"Thanks." Haley holds her head a little higher and Paige gives her a thumbs-up as she proceeds on down the red carpet.

"That really was a great dress," Paige tells me as I move in closer. "And I suspect that Haley Bernard has a bright future ahead. It's very cool that she went with vintage Chanel—very classic design, and yet it's perfect for a younger woman because it shows her off more than the dress." Paige laughs to herself. "In fact, you'd look great in a dress like that, Erin. Too bad I couldn't talk you out of your camera-girl clothes tonight." Then, since there's a break in celebs, Paige begins to do a commentary on my outfit, which turns out to be pretty funny. Fortunately, I'm used to my sister's fashion jabs, so I can take it, and I joke around with her for the cameras.

Then, to Paige's delight, Heidi Klum comes our way. Rather than getting nervous and starstruck, Paige calmly yet enthusiastically compliments Heidi on her gown. "That has to be Armani," Paige says with confidence.

"Wow, you are good," Heidi tells her, then points to Paige. "You look stunning too. Is that Armani?"

Paige nods. Heidi soon moves next to Paige. "Get a shot of the two of us together—both in Armani!" I get down low and take some shots. Heidi and Paige take a moment to chat about fashion, and at the end Heidi actually offers to make a guest appearance on our show.

"That would be fantastic," Paige tells her. "You know, we'll be at Fashion Week in New York in February."

"I'll be there," Heidi says as prepares to move down the red carpet. "Give me a call."

"Thanks, I will." Paige looks like she wants to do the happy dance now. "Somebody pinch me," she quietly squeals. "I just met Heidi Klum!"

Heidi's appearance seems to be the beginning of a good run of celebrities. Paige interviews Jessica Alba in Valentino, Miley Cyrus in Versace, Jennifer Hudson in Dior ... and the list keeps growing. I'm thinking this is actually a lot of fun, and Paige is winning people over left and right with her fashion knowledge and enthusiasm.

Suddenly, I see Paige's expression change and her jawline tighten. I turn to see that Benjamin and Mia are now strolling our way, with arms linked together as if they're a couple again. I want to throw something. Benjamin's nose is still swollen, but with his sunglasses you almost wouldn't notice it. Mia actually looks really good in a pale-pink gown, and she is holding on to Benjamin's arm as if to say, "Look, I won the prize. He's mine, all mine!"

By the time I look back at my sister, she is cool and collected, smiling at the happy couple as she begins to talk. "It's Mia Renwick and Benjamin Kross—the stars of *Malibu Beach*, and old friends!" She winks for the cameras. "But I wonder ... will any punches be thrown here tonight?"

"I don't think so," Benjamin says with a smile that oozes charm.

"Mia, Mia," Paige says warmly. "You look gorgeous in that gown." She places a finger on her chin as if thinking. "Let me guess ... I think it's one of my favorite designer duos. Is it Badgley Mischka?"

Mia gives my sister a curt nod. "How *did* you know?" she says in a sarcastic tone.

"Just a lucky guess." Paige laughs. "But who would've guessed that one of America's favorite couples would be back together so quickly after the big breakup episode last week." She shakes her head. "Only in Hollywood, right?"

"Right," Benjamin mutters.

"And you, Benjamin," Paige continues. "What are you wearing?"

"You don't want to guess?" I can hear the teasing note in his voice.

"I'm not as good at guy fashion, but I must admit you look fabulous."

"Armani."

"What a coincidence," she says lightly. "I'm in Armani too. Armani Privé."

He clears his throat, then glances at Mia. "We should probably get in there ... it looks like it's getting late."

"Have fun!" Paige calls cheerfully. As they continue on their way, she continues to chatter at me. "Isn't it amazing how celebrities break up and make up and show up at the Golden Globes? It's enough to make your head spin, isn't it?"

"The next thing you know Jennifer Aniston and Brad Pitt will walk in together," I say sarcastically.

Paige laughs. "Followed by Paul McCartney and Heather Mills." We banter like this for a few minutes, but it seems clear that the red carpet is pretty much over, or at least for us. "Should we pack it up?" Paige asks the camera crew.

"Wait until Fran gives us the green light," JJ tells her.

We continue to stand around, and Paige manages to keep her spirits up and the chatter coming. I suspect it's her way of distracting herself from the fact that Mia and Benjamin showed up here together. She rambles on about whose gown was the best and who looked the hottest, finally deciding that Jessica Alba in her Valentino should win the best-dressed award.

"How about worst dressed?" I ask.

She looks at me and frowns.

"Never mind," I say. "I know the answer to that question."

Fran finally comes over and tells us that it's time to wrap it up. Paige puts on a big smile as she poses for the camera crew. "Well, there you have it," she says cheerfully, "the Golden Globes red carpet. I don't know when I've had so much fun. Now remember—always put your best foot forward." She sticks out a delicate, pearly sandal and grins. "And tonight that would be Prada! See you all at the Oscars next time. This is Paige Forrester for *On the Runway*."

"That's a wrap," Fran tells everyone.

Paige looks relieved and weary as she removes her mic. "Are you okay?" I ask quietly as I help her to extract the wiring from the back of her dress and hand it to the sound technician.

"Yeah." She nods. "I'm fine."

"Were you pretty shocked to see them together?"

"On some levels."

"I guess Benjamin's just showing his true colors."

"I guess ..." She's still smiling, but her eyes are sad.

I wish there was something I could tell her, something to make her feel better. But I'm so mad at Benjamin right now, I would probably say something really mean. And why go there?

"Oh … no …" Paige's eyes get wide as she hands Fran back a diamond earring.

"Did you lose one?" I ask in alarm, hoping they're insured.

"No." She's looking behind me, and I turn to see Benjamin walking toward us. What is he planning to do — rub it in some more? What is this guy's problem? Besides being selfish and two-faced.

"Can I talk to you, Paige?" he asks quietly.

She hands the second earring over to Fran, who is now looking on with curious interest. We're all watching. It reminds me of seeing a wreck alongside the highway; you know you should look away, but you can't take your eyes off of it.

"Shouldn't you be inside for the awards show?" Paige asks.

"I'm not going."

"Not going?"

He shakes his head. "No. I was forced to escort Mia here by our producer. But that's the end of it. They can't make me sit by her all evening. Not when I want to be with you."

Paige looks surprised. I think we all do.

"You guys go on without me," she says quickly. Then, just like that, she and Benjamin take off. I'm standing here wondering, what just happened?

"Young love," Fran says as she picks up her oversized bag and drops the jewelry case inside. "You ready to go, Erin?"

I nod as I slip my camera into my backpack. "Sure." But I'm still trying to wrap my head around this. Benjamin shows up with Mia while the press is here and cameras are rolling … then after everything quiets down, he sneaks out and leaves with Paige. What is wrong with that picture?

When we get back to the studio, I realize that Paige drove us here. I am carless. I try Mollie first, but it goes straight to voicemail. So next I call Blake, who sounds pleased to hear my voice and gladly offers to come get me.

As soon as I'm in his car, I spill the whole story. "I just don't get it," I say. "Why would she go with him like that? After everything he's done to her? Why would she give him the time of day?"

"Because she really likes him?"

"But why?"

"You'd have to ask her." Blake stops for a light. "Think about it, Erin. He walked out of the Golden Globes just to be with her. That's gotta be worth something, don't you think?"

"Maybe." Still, I'm not convinced. "I just don't trust him," I confess, "and I don't think Paige should either."

"Maybe she wants to give him a second chance."

"He doesn't deserve one."

"So what's really bugging you here, Erin?"

"What do you mean?"

"Why are you so angry about this?"

I think about that. "I'm not sure. I mean, I do feel protective of Paige, and I resent how Benjamin just strolled in and took her away."

"Are you jealous?

"Not exactly." I'm trying to be honest with myself now. "But maybe I felt a little pushed aside by my sister. We've been through a lot lately. And Benjamin has seriously hurt her. I'm not sure."

"You can't control your sister's life, you know."

I look down. "Yeah . . . I know."

"And she's got her eyes wide open this time. She knows who Benjamin is and what he's capable of . . . both good and bad."

"You're right." I lean back and sigh. "I need to let it go, don't I?"

"Maybe so ... but at least you can put it in God's hands." He brightens. "Okay, now tell me how it went tonight. How did Paige do? And who did you girls talk to?"

I begin recapping our interviews, and Blake is a good listener. By the time he drops me at home, I don't feel quiet as grumpy as I did when he picked me up. "Thanks," I tell him. "You are really a good friend."

He just nods like that's not exactly what he wanted to hear.

"And if it makes you feel any better, I've been considering upping you to more than just a friend."

"Oh yeah?" His eyes light up.

"I'm thinking about it."

When I get to the condo, there's a note from Mom reminding us that she's at Jon's house for a Golden Globe party, but that she recorded the show so that we can watch it from the beginning. I turn on the TV and sit there, watching blankly, then realize it's not much fun watching it by myself so I turn it off. As I sit there, I start thinking about Paige again. As much as I want to let this thing go, it's hard. I'm worried that she's just opened herself up to more heartache. Seriously, who knows what that boy will pull next week? He's flakier than a croissant.

"Hey, Erin," Paige calls as she comes into the house. "What's up?"

"I'm surprised you're back this soon," I tell her.

"Why?"

I shrug, then turn the TV back on.

"Are you mad at me?"

I shrug again. "Want to watch the Golden Globes?"

"Not until we talk." She takes the remote and turns off the TV. "What's wrong, Erin?"

"I just feel kind of confused."

"About Benjamin and me?"

I nod. "He's kind of bouncing back and forth, don't you think? I guess I'm afraid he's going to jerk you around again."

She sits down with a thoughtful look. "I think he's been jerked around some too ... by Mia and his producers. But I also think that I've learned a thing or two in the last week."

"Such as?"

"Such as I'm very lucky to have you as my little sister."

"Really?" I blink in surprise.

"And I've learned that I need to make room in my life for things like God and praying."

"Really ..." I try not to look overly stunned, but this is news to me.

"Yes. I'm not saying that I'm going to start going to church all the time like you seem to enjoy doing. But I'm open to some things. That night I was out walking in the rain and feeling a little hopeless ... well, it was kind of like an awakening. Sort of a rude awakening. I probably needed something like that to get my attention."

"That's cool, Paige."

"And this thing with Benjamin ... well, I have no idea where it will go, or if I even want to give it a try. I told him I still needed time, but that I'll think about it. That's about all I could offer."

"Sounds reasonable. So did he go back to the Golden Globes?" I ask.

"He said he was going home."

"Wow ... that's pretty amazing. I mean, that he gave that up for you."

She nods as she turns on the TV, rewinding the awards show back to the beginning. "You ready for this?"

"Sure. I'll make popcorn." I hop up and head for the kitchen. And before long, we're just regular sisters again, sitting around in our sweats and eating junk food and watching the Golden Globes together. Paige starts commenting on gowns that she hadn't seen earlier and she's picking out the worst and the best, and we're laughing and joking. It's hard to believe that just a couple of hours ago, we were standing on the red carpet and filming our own TV show.

Finally the last award has been presented and Paige stands up and stretches. "What a night," she says.

"And in case I forgot to mention it," I tell her, "you were great on the red carpet. It's amazing how easy all that comes to you. I would've been tongue-tied from the get-go."

Paige hugs me. "Maybe so, little sister. But don't kid yourself. I couldn't do it without you. And, please, don't even think about quitting the show."

"Don't worry, I'm not." I point my finger in the air. "On to the Oscars!"

"And to Fashion Week in New York!"

I grin. "And who knows, maybe next year it will be Paige Forrester actually attending the Golden Globes, maybe even as a nominee."

"Paige and Erin Forrester," she adds.

I laugh. "Yes, I can just see you in a glamorous gown, and I'll have on my photographer's outfit of cargo pants and—"

"No, you'll have on Versace."

"And my safari vest with—"

"No, Valentino!"

We laugh and head for bed, but before I go to sleep, I remember to thank God for whatever it is he's doing in my sister ... and in me.

DISCUSSION QUESTIONS

1. Paige and Erin, though sisters, are very different from each other. Which character do you relate more to? Why?

2. Paige, like many young women, adores fashion. Why do you think that is? What is your attitude toward fashion?

3. How would you describe your fashion image? (Haute couture? Classic cool? Trendy chic? Practical sporty? Earth friendly? Frump frau? Clueless? Or something completely different?)

4. Erin signs on to participate in *On the Runway* with some reluctance. If you were her friend, what might you say to her? How would you advise her about her decision?

5. Why do you think reality TV is so popular these days? Do you think it has a positive or negative influence on viewers? Why do you feel this way?

6. Early in the story, Erin seems to still be suffering from a broken heart. Why do you think she took the breakup with Blake so hard? Can you relate to her?

7. Paige and Erin's mom (Brynn) is widowed. How do you think this has impacted their family? What do you think of Brynn's parenting skills?

8. What was your initial reaction when Blake came back into Erin's life? Do you agree or disagree with Erin's response to Blake? Explain.

9. Describe your first impression of Benjamin. After you finished the book, did your opinion change at all? Explain why you felt the way you did.

10. What would you say to Paige regarding Benjamin? (And do you think she would listen?)

11. Why do you think Paige and Erin's relationship is strained at times? Is there anything that you'd like to tell these sisters?

12. If there's such a thing as "fifteen minutes of fame," describe what you would like yours to be like.

A NOVEL

Catwalk

On the Runway

Melody Carlson

Bestselling Author

Chapter

1

"*Now, this is what I'm talking about!*" I point to the building as Paige and I get out of her car. The entire front of this three-story boxlike structure is covered in a massive collage (made with recycled soda cans) depicting what I think must be a rhinoceros, standing beneath some palm trees and a colorful rainbow. "Seriously." I squint up at the shiny image. "How cool is that?"

"Right ... and if that's considered art, I can only imagine what the inside will look like." Paige shakes her head as we approach the old building. "I cannot believe Helen put this one on the list."

Unlike my sister, I know exactly why this design studio's on the list. And I'm glad for it. I've had it up to my eyeballs with all the slick uptown studios, those overly serious designers and their stick-thin models. I cannot wait to meet this particular designer. Because Granada Ruez is a *real* person—and she designs for *real* women. I've been a fan of her environmentally conscious clothing for several years now.

Last week, when Granada won an international design

award for humanitarian efforts in Third World countries, I brought it to our producer's attention. Paige may not know it, but I'm the reason we're here today. I'm the one who convinced Helen Hudson that *On the Runway* needed to feature Granada Greenwear on our local designers episode.

"This feels like a mistake," Paige says as she opens the door.

"Granada Greenwear may not be considered high fashion," I tell my sister as we enter the showroom, "but we need to give her a chance." I'm trying to contain my enthusiasm because I know it will only aggravate Paige. She's already dragging her heels.

As if to emphasize the fact that she's not into recycled clothing, Paige dressed to the nines this morning—and she's wearing a designer who recently made fashion headlines for his blatant disregard of certain environmental issues. "But his style is superb and his clothes are perfectly timeless," Paige told me after I pointed out her faux pas. She is so out of touch.

"We're here to see Granada Ruez," I tell the salesgirl inside. "I'm Erin Forrester and—"

"I'm Paige Forrester from *On the Runway*." Paige holds out her business card, taking over as if being here was all her idea in the first place.

"Oh, right." The girl peers curiously at us. "Hey, didn't I see you two on *Malibu Beach*—the breakup episode?"

"Yes, but that's not our show." Paige points to the card. "We're *On the Runway*. Have you seen it?"

"Not yet."

"Well, maybe you'll want to tune in ... in case we decide to include today's interview." Paige's smile fades from bright to tolerant now. And I give her a look that says *just be nice!*

"In that case, I'll be sure to watch it," the girl says.

"Our director and production crew should be here shortly," Paige informs her. "In the meantime, do you mind if we look around your shop and put together some kind of attack plan?"

I frown at my sister, worried that she means that literally. Hopefully she doesn't plan to attack Granada Ruez.

"Sure. I'll tell Granada you're here. By the way, I'm Lucinda." She then points to me. "And you're wearing a Granada Green jacket. One of the earlier designs."

"I got it a couple of years ago and I still love it. It's so comfortable."

"Cool." Lucinda smiles as she heads for a door in back.

"Right ... *cool*." Paige rolls her eyes at me. "You know how much I hate that jacket, Erin."

"Be quiet," I warn.

"It's frumpy and not the least bit flattering."

"Are you going to keep this up?" I glance to the back of the showroom to be sure no one is listening.

She shrugs. "Hey, don't forget this is my show and it's supposed to be about fashion and style." She pulls a recycled denim dress from a rack, holding it out at arm's length as if she's afraid it might bite her. "And this does not even come close to being fashionable or stylish. Good grief, no one—not even Kate Moss—could make this rag look good."

"Paige!" I hiss at her.

"Sorry, but you know how this gets to me, Erin."

"Just try to be polite, *please*."

"Fine, I'll be politely honest." She puts the dress back and sighs. "But I can't promise you that Granada Greenwear will get a spot on the show. Unless I use it in my *fashion don'ts* segment."

"Why can't you think positively?" I ask. "What about protecting the environment or fair treatment of overseas workers? Both are issues that Granada respects and fights for. Doesn't that mean anything to you?"

"Of course." Paige nods. "You know I'm totally for that. But it's too bad Granada's focusing her efforts in the *fashion* industry." Paige pulls out a baggy-looking pair of drawstring pants and frowns. "She might be better off making home décor products. Like this fabric would be nice for, say, a couch slipcover." She chuckles. "And these pants are almost big enough."

"Those pants look comfortable to me." I take them from her and feel the fabric. "See how soft this is." I read the label. "Bamboo fibers," I tell her. "A renewable resource with very little negative impact on the planet."

"The negative impact comes when someone walks down the street wearing those hippo pants." She laughs. "Hey, I think I'll use that line on the show."

"Maybe we should just forget the whole thing." I put the pants back on the rack. "If you're going to make fun of Granada Ruez, I refuse to be involved."

"So you want to leave then? Just make some excuse and get out of here?"

I just shrug, feeling totally deflated.

Now Paige almost looks contrite. "Hey, I'm sorry, Erin," she says quietly. "I got carried away. I didn't mean to rain on your parade."

"Yeah ... well ... not everyone is into your brand of *haute couture* style. Some of us are quite happy to be comfortable and environmentally aware. Why can't *On the Runway* cater to those types too? I just read that there's going to be an earth-friendly design show during Fashion Week in New York. They seem to get the importance of it, and I, for one, plan to be there for it."

"I've got it!" Paige exclaims.

"What?"

"You can do the Granada Greenwear interview yourself. And you can be our *On the Runway* conservation expert. That way I won't sound like a complete hypocrite by giving my thumbs-up to bad style."

"But I'm supposed to be *behind* the camera, remember?"

"It's your choice, Erin. If you want to pursue this idea of green fashion, you'll have to do it in *front* of the camera." She holds up a patchwork shirt and just shakes her head. "Because I simply cannot force myself to pretend that I like this granola wear."

We hear laughter from behind us and I turn to see Granada and Lucinda standing nearby. "Did you just hear all that?" I ask lamely.

Granada nods. "And don't worry, it's not the first time I've experienced that reaction. I'm fully aware that Granada Greenwear is not for everyone. We don't even want to be." Granada is Demi Moore meets Whoopi Goldberg — or maybe I'm thinking of the old film *Ghost*. But she has delicate features, expressive eyes, and these wild-looking brown dreadlocks that reach halfway down her back. And, although she's a lot more bohemian than I could ever be, she's very stylish.

"I *love* your clothes," I say in all earnestness.

"But your sister does not." Granada frowns as she takes in Paige's outfit. "And unfortunately you appear to love designers who *don't* love our planet. Why is that?" She comes closer and looks into Paige's eyes. "Do you like the idea of small children working ten hours or more a day, seven days a week, in disgusting conditions, just so you can wear those fancy clothes? Or perhaps you don't mind that toxic fabric dyes and chemicals—the ones used to make your pretty little outfit—contribute to the harmful runoff that pollutes waterways and wildlife? Some of the very water sources that the poor need just to survive? Is that the price you think should be paid just so someone like you can look *chic*?"

Paige, for once in her life, is speechless.

"I told her not to wear that outfit," I say to Granada.

Granada just smiles. "I'm sure she only wore it to get my hackles up. And it's worked."

"I wish I had my camera on while you were talking," I tell Granada. "Paige is usually the one dishing out the criticism!"

She waves her hand. "I say things like that all the time—especially when I'm talking to the skeptics."

"I don't mind protecting the planet," Paige finally says. "I just won't call something unattractive stylish."

"But don't you think style, like beauty, is in the eyes of the beholder?" Granada gives Paige a quick head-to-toe glance.

"Yes, I suppose you're right." Paige stands a bit straighter. "But *On the Runway* is my show, so I guess that makes me the beholder. And, I'm sorry, but I wouldn't be caught dead in these clothes."

Fortunately Granada just laughs again.

"But what if someone died making your clothes?" I challenge my sister.

Her brow creases. "Well, that would make me sad. But I don't think that's really the—"

"Don't be so sure," Granada tells her. "In fact, why don't you check out my website to see for yourself? I have a number of articles there about pollution and inhumane practices in foreign countries. You might be surprised at what goes on ... all in the name of fashion."

I turn to Paige. "I think I'll take you up on your offer. I would like to interview Granada myself."

"I can't promise you that it'll air," Paige tells me. She nods to the front door where Fran, our director, and the rest of our crew are just coming in. "But you can give it your best shot and see what Helen says when she sees it."

And that is exactly what I do. For the next hour I interview Granada about her design work as well as her concern for the planet. Paige even helps me to rephrase some questions so they come out better. And then we actually film a conversation between Granada and Paige, very similar to the one they had earlier. My sister cooperates, playing the shallow fashionista (complete with her witty pokes at bad style and her ignorance about green issues) as Granada educates her about some atrocities going on in other countries.

When I'm done with the interview two things surprise me: First, I pulled this interview off, being comfortable in front of the camera instead of hiding behind it. Second, Fran seems to think that me as *Runway's* conservation expert could be a good segment.

"I have an invitation for you," Granada tells me as we're packing up to go.

"What's that?"

"Come be in my fashion show next week."

"Me?" *Okay, this woman must be really desperate for models.* "Uh, did you notice my height?"

She laughs. "My models are from all walks of life, Erin. You are a beautiful girl and you would fit in perfectly. Trust me."

Paige lets out a giggle and it's not hard to guess what she's thinking.

"Fine," I say in aggravation. "I'll be in your fashion show. And I'll ask our producer if we can film some of it for our show."

"That'd be great." Granada hands me a brochure. "As you can see we have some well-known models participating too. Everyone's time is being donated because the proceeds are going to FIFTI."

"Fifty what?" Paige asks in interest.

"F-I-F-T-I," Granada explains. "Fashion in Fair Trade Industries. We used to have fifty members, but thankfully we've gotten even bigger."

"Oh?" Paige points to a name on the brochure I'm holding. "Is Sunera really going to be in your show?"

"Of course." Granada nods.

"Who's that?" I ask.

"One of the top models in the industry," Paige informs me. "She was born in Nigeria. Totally gorgeous. Internationally famous. Just about the hottest thing in fashion."

"She's flying in from Paris just for this event," Granada says.

Paige is still studying the brochure. "You have quite a lineup here."

"All women who care about fair trade and preserving the planet."

"Some of them are a bit past their prime," Paige says, "but impressive all the same." She hands me back the brochure now. "You *are* in good company, Erin."

Suddenly all my insecurities kick in. "I don't know," I say to Granada. "Maybe it's not such a good idea for me to model for your show. I mean, I've never done anything like that before and I'm totally inex—"

"Nonsense," she tells me. "You'll be great."

I glance at Paige, wishing she'd save me from myself. "You'll be fine, Erin," she says in a congenial way. "In fact, it'll be good for you."

"Hey, why don't you do it too?" I suggest hopefully. "It could be Paige Forrester from *On the Runway* actually *on* the runway."

Paige laughs. "I seriously doubt that Granada would want me for her—"

"Don't be so sure." Granada holds a finger in the air. "In fact, I am getting an idea . . . or perhaps it's more of a challenge."

"What?" Paige almost looks interested.

"You seem convinced that green fashion equals bad fashion, right?"

Paige shrugs with a coy expression, like, duh, the answer is obvious.

"So how about if I put together an outfit that I think you'd actually *want* to wear—I mean out in public. And if you like it well enough, you must agree to model it in my fashion show."

"Do you think that's even possible?" Paige frowns. "I've looked around your shop and I'm sure your clothes appeal to *some* people. But I'm not exactly an earth muffin, you know."

"I know." Granada seems to be thinking. "But I'd like to prove that green fashion can be high fashion."

"Just keep in mind that I've got a reputation to maintain," Paige says. "I'm known for being bluntly honest when it comes to style. And I refuse to act like I love some eco-fashion outfit when I really don't."

"Are you willing to give it a try?"

Paige seems to be considering it. "Sure. Why not?"

So they shake hands and it's like the green gauntlet's been

thrown. And while I like that Paige is giving this a fair shot, I'm worried for Granada's sake. I know my sister's influence is growing. What if Paige humiliates Granada on our show? And, if she does, will it be my fault? Will I be to blame if green fashion goes backward in the minds of some of our viewers?

Carter House Girls Series
from Melody Carlson

Mix six teenage girls and one '60s fashion icon (retired, of course) in an old Victorian-era boarding home. Add boys and dating, a little high-school angst, and throw in a Kate Spade bag or two ... and you've got the Carter House Girls, Melody Carlson's chick lit series for young adults!

Mixed Bags
Book One

Stealing Bradford
Book Two

Homecoming Queen
Book Three

Viva Vermont!
Book Four

Lost in Las Vegas
Book Five

New York Debut
Book Six

Spring Breakdown
Book Seven

Last Dance
Book Eight

Pick up a copy today at your favorite bookstore!

Visit **www.zondervan.com/teen**

Lonely? Jealous? Hurt?
Melody Carlson addresses the
issues you face today.

The TrueColors Series

The TrueColors series addresses issues that most affect teen girls. By taking on these difficult topics without being phony or preachy, best-selling author Melody Carlson challenges you to stay true to who you are and what you believe.

9781576835296

Dark Blue
(Loneliness)
9781576835296

Faded Denim
(Eating Disorders)
9781576835371

Deep Green
(Jealousy)
9781576835302

Bright Purple
(Homosexuality)
9781576839508

Torch Red
(Sex)
9781576835319

Moon White
(Witchcraft)
9781576839515

Pitch Black
(Suicide)
9781576835326

Harsh Pink
(Popularity)
9781576839522

Burnt Orange
(Drinking)
9781576835333

Fool's Gold
(Materialism)
9781576835340

Blade Silver
(Cutting)
9781576835357

Bitter Rose
(Divorce)
9781576835364

9781576835319

9781576835302

9781576835364

Coming in April 2011: Book 2 in the Secrets series.

To order copies, call NavPress at
1-800-366-7788, or log on to
www.navpress.com

NAVPRESS